THE EMANCIPATION OF KAT TURNER

ROB COOKE

Published in U.S.A.

This paperback edition published 2023

ISBN:

ACKNOWLEDGEMENT

Thank you to Kyra, Kevin and Daniel.

Thank you to Gloria Ogo and GO Edits for their editing services.

I

Chapter 1

In the tense interior of the Baptist church that Sunday morning, Uncle Zeke stood from his chair. With a hard gaze fixed on the congregation, his firm thumb and forefinger reached up to adjust the knot of his tie.

Not a soul expressed surprise when Uncle leapt in front of the pulpit and launched into a tirade. "The US government is trying to end an institution down here in the South. We need to protect our Christian values."

Anxious hand-fans flapped the heated air. Everyone waited. Not even a cough. This was exactly what they wanted to hear.

Uncle Zeke had their attention. He knew his way around a crowd, so he jumped in front of the congregation seated at the front pews of the outdoor tent that masqueraded as a church. His thick, baritone boomed across the heated tent and all the way to the flock at the back. No one escaped Uncle Zeke's tirade once he had his mind set on it. He jumped up and down, down the aisle and all around with his thumb stuffed in between the page of his new leather Bible.

"Let us all turn our pages to Ephesians Chapter 6. We will begin from verse 5 and read all the way through 7." He pranced one more time, giving his audience enough time to flip to the correct page. "Everyone there?" he asked.

A chorused affirmative from the crowd acknowledged his question. With a satisfied nod, he jumped back on the pulpit and opened his Bible.

"It says right here, everyone read along." Uncle Zeke moved with ease, even though my father's brother was fatter than my Quaker abolitionist father.

Still caught up in the throes of the moment's excitement, Uncle Ezekiel jumped back down and made his way right to the middle of the gathering. From my seat at the back, I caught a good view of the sermon, and though it wasn't anything I wanted to hear, I had no choice but to sit it out.

My uncle continued to perform his magic of mesmerizing his audience. "Right here, right here," he screamed. "Everyone read aloud."

EPHESIANS, VI, 5-7: "SERVANTS, BE OBEDIENT TO THEM THAT ARE YOUR MASTERS ACCORDING TO THE FLESH, WITH FEAR AND TREMBLING, IN SINGLENESS OF YOUR HEART, AS UNTO CHRIST; NOT WITH EYE-SERVICE, AS MEN-PLEASERS; BUT AS THE SERVANTS OF CHRIST, DOING THE WILL OF GOD FROM THE HEART; WITH GOOD WILL DOING SERVICE, AS TO THE LORD, AND NOT TO MEN: KNOWING THAT WHATSOEVER GOOD THING ANY MAN DOETH, THE SAME SHALL HE RECEIVE OF THE LORD, WHETHER HE BE BOND OR FREE."

"Know what this means? We cannot let those Yanks interfere with our institutions. We know better and know what we must do. We'd rather fight for our way of life."

I snuck out as soon as the service was over, making good my escape all the way out of the door and from that spot turned to catch a last glimpse of Uncle Zeke still prancing around the pulpit, mingling with the attendees, and listening to the parishioners, landowners, and slaveholders scream

8

'Amen' in unison. I mounted my pony and rode off towards his plantation, a modest mass of acres where I spent every other Sunday aiding my cousins, Josiah and Cletus, on learning the plantation operations.

Today, Josiah and Cletus had stayed back at home to check over the books. Josiah, my eighteen-year-old cousin, was two years older than me and a bookworm. He was blessed with a knowledge of business and trained me on the operations. My father wanted me to attend the church service even though he disagreed with his older brother's beliefs. Yet for some reasons, the old man had insisted that a well-rounded foundation of the knowledge of The Lord would benefit me.

To be fair, my father was right, since my focus on visiting the plantation was Kat, one of Uncle's slaves. I thought her the prettiest girl in Louisiana, and she always gave me a shy smile each time she caught me stealing glimpses of her. I had thoughts about her; not immoral thoughts, but as Uncle Ezekiel's sermons became inflamed, another idea sketched itself on my mind.

Josiah strolled up in his usual slow, unhurried manner to meet me as my pony pranced near the slaves' quarters, searching for my love before my cousin did his tutoring.

"Robert, you didn't see Cletus anywhere?" Josiah raised an eyebrow, his expression inscrutable.

"I didn't see him. Then again, you know who I was looking for."

Josiah looked around. "She always takes her bath around noon. I figure that's why you sneaked out of Father's service early." His lips settled into a crooked grin.

I returned the smile and shoved my chin towards the bath shed. "She's in there?"

I dismounted and hitched my steed. Without waiting for an answer, I sprinted back to the cabins and hid in my usual spot from where I caught glimpses of Kat's teenage body. My breath caught at the sight of that slim figure that never goes away from my mind. Watching her scrub her sleek body got me thinking harder about my scheme. Though, if I could summon the courage to steal my uncle's property, my becoming pilloried was possible if caught. Knowing Uncle Zeke and his stupid pride, the man might even have me lynched, executed or hung like some damn Jesus on a cross. The more I watched her bathe, the more I knew I had to plan.

Kat snuck out from the tank where my uncle's slaves took their baths and glanced towards where I hid. I could see her eyes, soft and clear. She winked and flashed a quick smile before continuing towards the cabin. This was the third straight visit I had caught an eyeful of her alongside an impeccable view of those delicious things sixteen-year-old boys want to see on girls. Her round breasts were firm and growing and her bottom reminded me of the succulent peaches my father and I bartered for.

Kat thought she was fifteen. There was something about this my uncle's precise property that made me want to free her and make her mine. Of course, the laws made this intention illegal. I couldn't marry a person's property and, according to the laws of Louisiana, Kat wasn't human. She was solely to be bought and sold like a cotton gin, or the pecans Zeke's land produced.

Uncle Zeke's plantation bought and sold human equity. Keeping track of the assets was Josiah's job. A chore my cousin disdained. After Kat disappeared into the slaves' quarters, I snuck back into my uncle's house.

"Robert, welcome back. Did you catch a glimpse?" Josiah had a curious look on his face.

I nodded and then frowned. "Yeah, I need a plan. I got to do something about my feelings for Kat, talk with my father about this. I know he knows people who can help us."

Josiah's eyes opened wide, his mouth ajar. After a moment, in which he studied and weighted my seriousness on the subject, he asked, "Are you thinking about Mexico? Texas is a big state and crossing The Sabine will be nothing but crossing Texas will be a challenge. You need a foolproof strategy. You know about me and Millie? I've been thinking about riding off with her."

Millie, like Josiah, was seventeen, and I knew they were getting together. I once stumbled upon a romp of theirs, but never knew he loved her this way. I had assumed he was granting her favors instead of a whipping and in return, took liberties with the girl.

"So, you're not just playing with her?"

"Hell no! I'd be just like my scumbag father. He caught me banging her, and I had to lie to him. Told him she was helping another girl escape." Josiah glanced around to ascertain no overseer lingered within earshot He lowered his voice. "Millie had nothing to do with the escape. It was Clete. My little brother been stealing Pa's girls. At least the ones his age."

"Cletus? He's just a kid."

"Yeah. Unbelievable, right? You know he's more devious than you and me combined. He's got a hide-out down by the river. I asked you if you saw him the time you rode in, because if he's not around he's headed to the river, probably stole some young slave girl. To cover his tracks, I fudge Pa's books, so he doesn't know one's missing. Here, let me show you how I do it."

Josiah showed me the ledgers. He added money for the loss to make it look like the brothers were responsible for selling the lady. Their preacher father didn't pay enough attention to the goings on within this inherited plantation that my grandfather use to own. While Uncle Zeke got all the property, the land, buildings, and human labor, my father, because of his beliefs, refused all property and had instead

11

built a small three-room cabin situated a day's ride away and near the Sabine. Josiah told me Cletus's hideout is near our cabin. I have seen nothing but some old cypress trees and a few little caves but wouldn't think anyone would hide out with the prowling reptiles.

"I want to learn to ride like you, Robert. If we're going to do this, I must ride like the wind. You still visiting the Caddo on your way home?"

"Oh yeah, Pa is a friend of theirs. He Christianized them so they would not have to move off their land."

"Aren't they still practicing the old religion?"

"Yeah, but they still show up at my Pa's church to make it look good. It keeps them on the land they lived on for centuries. Pa doesn't want them to move, not like Grandpa and your pa."

"I don't want them to move either. Not sure why you, me and your pa think like we do."

"Well, you know my late Ma came from down south where da poor Creole's live. Mama always thought she was Creole but didn't know for sure, since she was raised in an orphanage."

"You think you got African or Injun blood in you then? Little wonder you ride like you do."

I grimaced and brushed aside his comment. "Got nothing to do with it. I just been riding and roping all my life. I had to just to survive."

"I need to learn to ride like you. Otherwise, I can never keep up. Take me down to the Caddo."

"Riding like me takes confidence and getting to know your horse. Best thing you can do is steal your pa's strongest horse. Remember, it's almost 600 miles to Mexico, so we need a horse with stamina. At first, we'll go riding, get used to him, and then push it as fast as hell."

12

"Stealing a good horse from Pa will be easy. He doesn't pay attention to his property. That's what the overseer is for, and we know he's a drunk, and so does my Pa. He's looking to replace him though." Josiah thumbed through some more of the ledgers he forged. "I can get that son-of-a bitch fired, but we need to watch him. He might suspect Millie and me on our relationship. His eyes are also on Kat. He thinks she's stealing from pa as well as trying to deflower her."

"She can't be stealing. She's too pretty to be a thief, but we will become bandits."

"There's been some household items missing and Pa thinks it's Kat. Plus, rumor has it he wants to sell her off within the month."

"Damn, we need to act fast. I need to talk to Pa. I'm heading home tomorrow and will be back next weekend."

"I guess I should be able to delay the sale, but Overseer Jenkins is unpredictable. The son-of-a-bitch might shackle her or Millie up and sell them off to a broker."

"Can we frame him for something?"

"Nah, right now Pa trusts him more than me. If we try to frame him, he will watch me closer. We need to be totally trusted to pull this off. Right now, the only ones I trust are Cletus, you and me. I'm sure your Pa we can trust. I know he knows folks."

The door slammed as my uncle Ezekiel Barnum entered his plantation home. Josiah and I remained in the office, examining ledgers. No longer could we discuss the escape. At least Kat would arrive back in the house. Kat's mother prepared the meals, while Kat helped her mother in the kitchen with serving and other kitchen duties, including cooking. I stuck around.

The two women served dinner in the late afternoon around 4:00 pm. Fried chicken, creamed corn, corn bread and sweet potatoes were on the menu. Cletus still had not arrived.

Josiah knew where he was, so I sat next to Josiah. Uncle was at the head of the table while his wife sat across from him on the opposite end. The youngest daughter sat across from my cousin and me. All but Josiah and I were in church clothes.

Kat brought the plates out and served my uncle first, scooping the creamed corn onto his plate with steady hands, then the sweet potatoes, followed by two hunks of chicken and a slab of cornbread. She circled the table, giving me occasional glances, winks, and smiles. She gave the men two pieces of golden cornbread and fried chicken, while the females only got served one. When Kat arrived to serve me, once again, she opened her mouth, exposing her not so perfect teeth. She flashed a pretty smile and slipped me a third slice of cornbread and an extra drumstick. Before I could comprehend what happened, she hurried off into the kitchen, hoping the extra grub went unnoticed by her owner.

Uncle Zeke may have been sloppy with keeping track of his inventory, trusting his oldest son to run the business, yet under his hawk-like eyes, he kept a tight knot on what happened within the house. I deftly pocketed the extra slices in a napkin and slipped them into my overalls pocket, but not fast enough. It didn't go unnoticed.

In the middle of scarfing our dinner, Uncle Zeke screamed. "Robert, why did that servant give you an extra drumstick and cornbread? Tell me in my office. March, boy, I will meet you there. Drop your food on the table."

My auntie attempted a protest, but the preacher muted her. "You don't mess with Ezekiel Barnum. She will pay later."

I marched into Uncle Zeke's office, where Josiah and I had fudged some of the financial books a few hours earlier and waited. One minute, then two passed while I stood over the mahogany desk looking out the window across the plantation, knowing I may get my punishment. I'd ride home if given the option. I could make it to the Caddo before dusk, if I took off now. I hoped for that option. I wasn't given it. The office door slammed, and in buzzed my father's brother.

He had with him my extra chicken leg and slab of cornbread and pointed them at me. "Why that nigger slave gives you extra slices? You ain't banging her are ya? You know she's special to this house."

"No, sir. I ain't doing nothing with her." I wondered what he meant by she's special to the house. I hope he meant she worked hard, and he wasn't corrupting her.

"Your aunt is speaking with her now. I know what your punishment is going to be. If I want to hire you on like you want, you need to be tough on dese niggers. I need to see if you can. Go finish your dinner and wait back in here once you are excused."

I did as I was told, since I needed to earn the fat man's trust. I returned to the dining room and finished the grub in solitude. Josiah and his younger sister were doing their post dinner chores, while my aunt and uncle discussed mine and Kat's punishment. My appetite was almost non-existent, so I was content to eat alone. Before I could finish my dinner, Uncle Zeke grabbed my arm and shoved me toward the back door. Kat already stood outside beside the Overseer Jenkins and his whip. There was no doubt he was going to strip her, and then whip her. I could only guess that my punishment was to witness the torture.

Overseer Jenkins led me and Kat to the sugar house. Wanting to be double sure she understood the fate that was about to befall her, he cracked his whip near her.

"Rip that dress off her!" the Overseer bellowed, then he snapped the whip in my direction. "Ya hear me? Rip it off, so we can see that ass of hers."

The bullwhip pointed at me, and only then did I realize my punishment. This wasn't a way to see a girl naked. It was nothing like the peeping I did as she bathed, when I wanted to hop in and scrub her petite body, and she'd wash me all over.

"Rip her dress off. I want to see her body. Stop stalling boy."

I tortured the girl more by stalling. She glanced at me and nodded. The soft eyes she often flashed at me in her naïve, flirtatious manor were now replaced by a hateful glare. Her lips protruded silently questioned my motives. I tried to say something but with my uncle and Overseer Jenkins in proximity, I was helpless. Action meant more than words anyway.

Poor thing realized her position, and from the way she stiffened her back to receive the lashes, I could tell this might have happened to her before. I grabbed her dress. I knew my place here as well, a hired hand nephew whose only purpose here was to get to know Kat better, earn her trust and steal my uncle's property. I reached for the back of her dress and clenched a good chunk of the fabric. I pulled on the cotton material harder than I wanted, ripped it in half and tossed her attire across the sugar house. Small scars were exposed on her back from previous beatings. They formed an "x" as well as a target for continued torture.

"You are a man after all." I heard my uncle shout in the background supervising the action. "See boy, it ain't that hard to whip dem slaves. Don't go loving them."

"Shove her down," Overseer Jenkins shouted. "Shove her to the ground!"

Kat stared me down, noticed my body shaking and her big brown eyes widened. The whites of her eyes looked too innocent. She sensed my hesitation, how much I didn't want to begin as Jenkins got ready to hand me the rope. His eyes tightened, and along with the redness that grew in his cheeks, his impatience grew. I saw the pistol in his holster and the fear of what the weapon could do to her propelled me into action. I shoved her to the ground face first. The hint of rope-burn scars running up her back were clear reminders that she's been here before. Then I noticed the whip and pistol in Jenkins's hand and holster. The bullwhip was presented to me.

"Don't look at him, Nigger!" Jenkins shouted. He'll go soft on you. It's hard to whip someone staring at ya."

Despite the need to earn the trust of the management, my uncle and Jenkins, I didn't want to whip her. Ripping her dress and shoving her to the ground was bad enough for the woman I intended to marry in Mexico. Chickening out or going crazy with the whip might ban me from accessing the plantation. Trust right now was essential, and all parties needed it. The whip now in my hand, I loosened my wrist. Still unable to speak, my eyes rested on my target. I did not focus on the middle of Kat's back, but on some rocks and twigs beside her naked body. I snapped the bullwhip, and a stone went flying. Kat screamed as the tails of the whip missed as if this was set up. I never miss a target; I could snap a pecan out of one of Uncle's trees. Roping and riding is what I do best.

Uncle Ezekiel waddled up to me, "Congratulations, Robert. Though you missed, I bet it taught both of you a lesson. This is a place of business, not an arena of fornication. I've seen the glances you two give each other and you both were disobedient. He placed his hand on my shoulder, firmly leading me away. "This is also a House of God, and one more thing my nephew, Peter 2.18 says, 'SERVANTS BE SUBJECT TO YOUR MASTERS WITH ALL FEAR; NOT ONLY TO THE GOOD AND GENTLE, BUT ALSO TO THE FROWARD.' You are not her master, and she is not your servant. I'm her master and she's my pretty servant girl. Remember that, and one more thing, Ephesians 6.5says 'OBEY YOUR EARTHLY MASTERS WITH FEAR AND TREMBLING, WITH A SINCERE HEART, AS YOU WOULD CHRIST.' "She knew who to serve and disobeyed my orders, and by accepting the additional food, you disobeyed me and God. Do you understand?"

I shrugged, then stared into his eyes. "Yes, sir," was all I could muster.

Kat turned her head to look back, her eyes searching for me. I saw Josiah nod in her direction. She stood about twenty feet from me now. I smiled at her, praying she knew I missed on purpose and a small grin appeared on her face before she picked up her ripped dress and dashed to her quarters, the dress not covering what it was supposed to.

Josiah sat on a bench carefully watching me stroll over to him. We hurried to the east edge of the house, where the sun reflected off the white picket fence and extended our shadows.

"You missed on purpose. I've seen you whip a water moccasin dead saving my sister."

"As long as I fooled Jenkins and your pa, I don't care. There wasn't no way I was hitting her. Stripping and shoving her was bad enough."

"You think she knows you missed on purpose?"

"I let her know. All of this for three pieces of chicken and an extra slice of cornbread."

We entered inside the house but did not speak. We waited for a servant to light the oil lamp, it flickering brightness chasing away the shadows of the descending sun in the western horizon.

Still not sure it was safe to speak, we climbed the stairs to Josiah's room, and there plotted the escape laying in our beds.

Josiah whispered, "Now we know what we're up against. Father keeps good track of what is under his nose. Jenkins is a monster, but also a drunk. They'll both be watching us now."

I responded, "We'll need a diversion, set something up heading north, leave clues of a fake escape to buy us enough time to get out of there. Once we're gone, they won't catch us, but I want a good day ahead of them."

"We need Cletus here. My little brother is deviant and sneaky."

"I don't trust him with all the details. We should also use him to mislead them. He can help with a diversion."

"He's my brother, we ain't setting him up."

"If we do it right, all five of us will be scot-free."

While Josiah appeared confused, my mind tried to figure this out if there were other pieces of the puzzle who had to keep silent. I thought of the families in Kat's quarters, Millie's quarters and the fact that we might need a sacrificial lamb. Cletus will have to come into play as a helper and a snitch.

"Your brother knows the land by the river better than me or my Pa. You say he has caves built that he uses?"

Josiah flipped sides on his bed and faced me again. "What are you getting at?"

"I'm not sure yet. We must have him help us west but make him think we're heading North even though he'll be with us in the caves."

"Got it." Josiah's voice resonated louder than it should. He caught his breath to relax. "Steamers. They roll up the Sabine.

Chapter 2

The next Sunday, I attended my father's church, a small service held in front of our cabin. The parishioners came from around the parish. Some Caddo and a few abolitionists in the area attended. Pa, nowhere as flamboyant as his older brother, circled the small congregation and spoke in a conversational tone to his audience.

"Let me quote you Galatians 5.1: 'FOR FREEDOM, CHRIST HAS SET US FREE; STAND FIRM THEREFORE, AND DO NOT SUBMIT AGAIN TO A YOKE OF SLAVERY.' I assume," he raised his voice an octave, nowhere near the fiery preaching of his older brother, "we are not to give in to the pressure of slavery. Also, for any person who is a slave, whether Native or African descent, resist. Fight back. God made us all human beings. We are in debt to one being, and that is God. God is your only master."

A younger male in his twenties attending with his wife stood up and raised his hand. He spoke with a Yank accent. "Pastor Barnum." He waited for my father to answer and then continued. "We are new to the area, and I recently attended a service by another Pastor Barnum. He spoke about slavery. Why does The Bible seem pro and against slavery? How do we know what to believe?"

My father took off his hat, scratched his head and circled his congregation again. He walked up to the man and knelt before him. "I'm a human first, then a pastor. Let me ask you in your heart. Do you think a man should own a fellow human being? Should he whip someone for mild disobedience? Should the owner rape his favorite female for his satisfaction? To me, that is adultery, and we know what this book says about infidelity. The Bible is filled with metaphors, and as human beings, we have evolved. When the book was written, we did not think with our hearts like we do now." Pa, still kneeling before the man, put his hand on his head and prayed for him. Once finished, the man shook his hand and joined us for dinner.

Father scratched his head again and then thumbed through his Bible. There have been several escapes in this area. What does God say? Well, right here in Deuteronomy, verse 23, paragraph 15. *'If a slave has taken refuge with you, do not hand them over to their master.'*

The gentleman interrupted. "So, we harbor a fugitive?" The man seemed unsure if this was the right or wrong thing to do. He waited for my father to answer.

"Never return them. Help them on their path, just like you would in one's spiritual path. My son, Robert," he pointed at me," has been reading up in Exodus, and I believe he knows why."

I nodded, even though I wasn't exactly sure. It was to appease father, but he gave me my Biblical lesson on the fly. I wasn't prepared. I didn't know my verses, and never memorized any.

"Robert," Father asked, "Exodus 20.2. What does it say?"

I pondered his question. Memorization wasn't my strong suit and I hoped Pa didn't want the exact quote. "I don't know the exact quote, but something like 'I'm God's messenger who will take you out of slavery'."

"That's close son, close enough where you got the message, but I will read for our honored guests. "*I am the LORD thy God, which have brought thee out of the land of*

Egypt, out of the house of bondage." He shut his good book and sat down at the table; his gaze fixed on me. I hadn't discussed my escape plans with him yet. Somehow, he knew.

Pa was a poor farmer, and we grew some crops on our small parcel of land for him and me. We grew fruits and vegetables and raised chickens. He fed the congregation on Sundays if we could, otherwise, it was a free-for-all. Then we encouraged the parishioners to bring meat or vegetables and we'd share our blessings. Another difference between my father's and uncle's church.

The attendees cleared out by late afternoon. My time with Father was running short. Within a month, I would head to Mexico with Kat, Josiah, and Millie on a mission. It was time for conversation.

I grabbed pails of water from the hearth and went on to meet Father outside, where we needed to scrub the utensils. We had little, so any pots needed scrubbed before the next meal. I rushed outside carrying the cast iron ware and eager to speak with my father.

"Pa, I need to talk to ya, plus I'm gonna need some help."

Father dropped the cutlery he used to chop the chicken into the pan of water that boiled in order to scrub it clean. He looked up. "What's up, Son?"

"You know I got a thing about that slave girl over at Zeke's?"

"Yeah, I figured you did. That's why you have been spending all your free time over there. What's up? Why, you need help?"

It was time to man up. My father was a compassionate man, soothing. He only whipped me when I deserved it. His voice wasn't monotone, he spoke with inflection and that made me uncertain about his true feelings to my words. "Josiah and I are going to take Kat and Millie to Mexico. We gonna do it in about a month and we just started planning.

You've told me about conductors on routes North to Ohio and further up to Canada. Anything similar going to Mexico?"

Father was more than an abolitionist preacher and farmer. He had contacts west of the river. Throughout the southern states, the movement was slight, and like the rest of the country, had to be discreet, only daring to share identities with one another. He finished the last chopping knife, tossed the pans in the water, and started scrubbing.

He looked at me, his face expressionless for a while, then he smiled. I wondered if he would try to scare me from our mission or knew how to pull off the escape. "Son," he removed his hat, "it's an awful risk. It's a federal crime for the girls, and also for you and Josiah. As I told you, the states' governments down here don't see these girls as young women, or even as humans. They are property, Zeke's property, and you know the punishment."

"Yeah, we were discussing it before I came back. We have some ideas. I know we can outrun them to the river. Thought about catching a steamer heading either direction, but we're not sure what to do with the girls or horses."

He picked up his hat and tugged on his suspenders. "You're a horseman, riding is your strength. Your best option remains to hide the girls in a wagon, blend in on the trail, and disguise your faces."

"Pa, I want to ride as hard as I can. I know Josiah and I can cut through the bayous around here. We can ride at night where no one can see us."

"There will be folks out searching for you. You know that. Finish scrubbing that pan, I got some maps stashed away with contacts. There are folks along the way that I trust 100 per-cent, some about 50, and others whom I'm aware with, so don't even go near those places. War is pending. Betrayal is common during pending battle and becomes more frequent during combat." He took a deep breath to calm himself, knowing that our days were numbered. "My first one is a two-day ride. Another factor is you'll be carrying another body. You'll slow up the horse a bit. Good news is they'll be tracking you with dogs. It will slow them down."

We finished the scrubbing and headed into our shanty. Father went to his roll-top desk and whipped out a Texas map. He flattened it out with a rolling pin. We had little, so Pa was good at improvising. The map was of East Texas, counties and towns scribbled on it with different colored dots.

"Are these conductors with the dots?"

"No, son. We can't take that chance. What I will tell you about it is the locations are a mile away from the dot on either side."

I sat down in his office chair, grabbed a magnifying glass and searched in the direction heading for Mexico. I saw a green-colored dot near Jasper. "Is this a place we can totally trust?"

"Yeah, green is one hundred per-cent safe. The yellow I'd trust as well. It's an easy four-day ride, three if you push it a bit."

He looked at me, smiling. "You're okay with me doing this, aren't you?"

"Taking those young women from your uncle would be the bravest thing you can do. You know I've helped Clete many times. Tomorrow, I'll take you out to the river and show you some things."

We finished our chores, and I made for my room. Once inside my little sanctuary, I lit a candle, and picked up a copy of a book I was earlier reading. "UNCLE TOM'S CABIN." I read until the southern breeze blew out the candle and I fell asleep.

The following day after some breakfast of bacon, biscuits and gravy that Father prepared, we packed up the steeds and rode west to the river. It was a good half-hour ride across the property, but one that passed with Father pointing hollowed out trees, caves, burrows and tunnels where my younger cousin had hidden prospective runaways, rafts, and even clothing.

"Your little cousin Cletus hangs out here. He can get you across the river. The kid has been doing this for years, sneaky little kid. The kid's got the same set-up over there." Father pointed to the west bank of The Sabine River, which separates Louisiana from Texas. The Cypress trees looked the same, eerie, places where no one would find us if we needed to hide from catchers.

I've hung out here a few times, noticed the swamp and swamp creatures, but never paid attention to the natural and dugout burrows, caverns, and the vegetation. I could stay down here for a night or two, become one with the creatures that roamed the swamps and the critters slithering through the bayou. If my younger cousin can become one with the animals, so could I. Josiah, Kat and Millie needed to trust them and we needed a leader since we might have to hide out for weeks underground, in silence, even if a water moccasin slithers by and bared its fangs.

Before we took the tour, we tossed fishing lines in the river to catch some channel cats for dinner. We had okra ready, and blackberries were abundant, so we'd eat dinner before heading back home.

We pulled in a five pounder and chopped the head off, and Pa skinned it. The skinless corpse of the fish flopped around before we gathered stones and sticks to set up a place to grill it. Dinner was a treat, since we used the last rooster on Sunday for our brunch we always hosted. Pa needed more chickens.

The next day I gathered what we could barter and took the buggy to the closest market to nab a couple of roosters. On the way, it hit me. Another month, my father would have no one to do his little errands for him. Ma has been gone for three years and I was an only child. I knew I'd be back; we would not live in Mexico forever, but when is what I wasn't sure about. What if a war broke out? I doubted anyone would shoot a man of the cloth. If they did, I'd fight against the side who killed my father. My time here was short. I needed a few days by the river and a few weeks at Uncle Zeke's. I needed Kat's trust, and we needed to plan an escape.

There were no chickens at the market, so me and the buggy trotted towards the Caddo, and passed more folks I'd miss. They were the ones who taught me to ride, and folks in the area knew no one could catch me. My native brothers were always good for a few chickens, so we could host our Sunday brunch. Something else I'd be missing.

"Robert Barnum, why you in the wagon?" the young shaman named John asked.

"My father and I ran out of birds to cook. Grilled the last one for brunch on Sunday. We need to gather up some more. I got some yams and maize to trade.

John stared me dead in the eyes. "There's a greater reason for you being here, Master Barnum. There's a reason the market was out. We have the birds, but you should seek your uncle first. He is blood and there is talk about a split. We must regain trust. Go seek your cousins and uncle."

I looked at him, mouth agape. Words must float down from my uncle's plantation on how I bailed whipping on Kat. "Pa needs some birds today."

"We will take your buggy and the chickens. Greater events are happening in the air that involve you. You must seek your uncle."

"Unhitch your pony, we will return it with the poultry desired. Your father, a man of wisdom, sent you on this journey. He believes in spirits greater than the White Man's Jesus. Go Robert. Your journey awaits." Before galloping off, the boys my age cleaned rabbits with flint, in preparation of the mid-day meal. I joined them in some rabbit and maize.

I arrived at Uncle Zeke's that evening in time for dinner. From the lack of surprise on their faces, I knew they were expecting me. Kat was not serving. I felt in my guts that something was up, Clete got caught, maybe somehow Uncle Zeke knew Josiah and my plans, or Cletus found out and tattled.

Then again, as the son of a preacher man, I was sure there was a lesson for me.

Chapter 3

When I retired to Josiah's room for the night, curiosity took over. I couldn't ask since Cletus was in the room. Cletus Barnum, Josiah's younger brother. Sneakier and devious than the two of us combined, learned at a young age how to play my father and Josiah against one another. I realized why I was here earlier than planned. I needed to lead. No one would be trustworthy, not Josiah, not Cletus, not Mildred or even Kat. Her family needed befriended, and Uncle Zeke needed my trust. At sixteen, I thought of myself as a man. I also thought I was just a kid, and as the son of a preacher, God was on our side. However, we'd be stealing from a reverend. I needed to sneak to the slave's quarters.

Overseer Jenkins' house sat on the other side from where Josiah and Cletus slept, however I had to sneak by his place to get to the cabins. Zeke had ten cabins two families per cabin. The overseer kept strange hours. He was often drunk. Hired as a middleman, his primary function was whipping the slaves when they needed disciplined. Uncle Zeke originally hired Jenkins to manage the operations, however, his incompetence forced Josiah into that capacity. A job Josiah disdained until he became an expert at creating false numbers.

Uncle Zeke's overseer kept unpredictable hours. We often saw him outside his home that was closer to the cabins than at the plantation home Zeke inherited. To get to Kat's cabin, I had to sneak by the man's modest home, one that was larger than the slave cabins but tinier than the giant house I stayed in while visiting my cousin and his kin.

Though taking the horse would be quicker, it would be noisier. The cabins were about two-hundred yards from the manager's place if I went direct. Three hundred if I took a safer route. I chose the latter. I knew which shanty was hers from spying on her bathing countless times. It wasn't her I sought, but her family.

Dogs' barks accompanied my sneaking across the fields with an occasional peeking over my shoulder. I could see the overseer's shadow through the flicker of the lantern. I dashed towards the cabins, counting fast. Her family's shack was the fourth building down, a two-room cabin. One room housed her family including Kat, her mother, father, and five siblings. The adjoining facility accommodated the Johnsons. Someone rumored the Johnsons to be snitches, and ones who accepted Uncle Zeke's sermons. I couldn't trust them. More counting placed Millie's cabin in the far end, closest to the bayou. I noticed it in the moonlight, a quarter moon passing through the clouds. We'd get her last, but it was still too soon- I prepared mental notes.

I tapped on the door, loud enough for Kat's family to hear the rapping, but not enough to raise suspicion next door. Kat nudged the door open, her eyes sparkled when she spotted me through candlelight. She opened it wide enough to let me slip inside their shanty. Once I was in, her eyes followed me as I approached her father. I strolled toward a tall, broad shouldered, dark skin man sitting on the floor plucking a musical instrument, made from a dried squash. He played with perfect rhythm and hummed a ditty that Kat's siblings sang along in quiet voices. I was unable to decipher the words before he strummed another tune. The family sang along,

"JUBA HIS AND JUBA THAT, JUBA CHASED A YELLOW CAT. JUBA UP AND JUBA DOWN, JUBA RUNNING ALL AROUND."

I inched forward as the family danced around the father. Still humming and singing, he flicked his fingers across the horsehair made up the strings. He finally acknowledged me at the end of the third quick tune.

"Mastah Barnum, what brings you here sneaking through the night?"

I led him to the furthest corner of the cabin, away from the rest and, of course, where the Johnsons could not eavesdrop.

"Mister Turner," I needed respect, and I always respected the man, plus it was best to ask the father's permission to marry his daughter. "I want to let you know something, some evening in the next month. I want to marry your daughter Katherine. I know I can't do it here. I'll take her to Mexico. My pa said we need to ask your permission."

He looked at his eldest daughter, then back at me. "You be risking my daughter's life and yours." His sincerity overwhelming.

"I'll risk everything to get her away from this place. I know it's the only home she's ever had, but you ain't living here. Zeke thinks you are nothing but property, but when I hang around here, I see people. I hear folks singing and playing music. Property doesn't play banjers, people do."

"You go take her. What about us? You be making us stay here. I know Mastah Zeke ain't as bad as others, and we know no other life. If you love my daughter, you also love her family."

I glanced around, wondering who might overhear the conversation. "I can get you to The Indian Nations, or maybe Canada. If you go North, there are paths along the way.

Plenty of people who think like my father down here, plus up yonder." I pointed in a Northern direction.

"I gots kinfolk who had been sold off, no longer living with us. I ain't got no idea where they be livin'."

"I can't promise anything about finding them or getting them to freedom, but I promise I'll get her to freedom." I gleamed at Kat's face in the candlelight. Her skin glistened as the light flickered. A smile then a tear formed in her eye before the candle flickered.

"When are you planning on doing this?"

"Soon, but I don't know when. It will be in another moon. Maybe sooner. I need to sneak back to the house. Josiah plans on taking Millie. Don't tell a soul."

"Only me and my God knows about this. I'll tell my daughter, but you will need to stay away. Mastah was already suspicious of things. Already put us in the fields, away from the house. Said something about her sneaking you an extra piece of bird, and then you not whipping her. Mastah Robert, you gonna earn Mastah Zeke's trust to pull this off. You can't be sneaking around here."

"I'm gonna sneak back, don't tell anyone, especially them folks in the next cabin."

"Yeah, they be Toms and I don't trust any single one of them."

"I got me an idea on them too, then." I shook his hand and glanced at Kat as I head to the door. Her father plucked his squash banjo again. Kat and I danced a jig before I snuck out. I dashed across the field and crawled back through Josiah's bedroom window.

"Where did you go?" he asked, arms stretched above his head and wiping the dust from his eyes.

I glanced around and didn't see his younger brother. "I went to her quarters and spoke with her father."

"You did what?" he whispered his scream.

I kept glancing around the room in search of his brother. "Two reasons, asking for permission, and I need to earn his trust. In addition, your father has his eye on me. He knows I missed whipping her on purpose and thinks something is going on. Where's Cletus?"

"Robert, I don't know. He might be at the river or sneaking around. He might even be talking to father. We can't talk about nothing in the house."

"We need him, don't we?"

"We shouldn't talk about this inside."

"A diversion, I got it. Clete leads them astray, her family boards a steamer heading North. Pa has maps."

"What are you talking about?"

"Two for one. Her family goes up the river, gets to the nations, while we ride free to the first conductor. If Cletus is a snitch, they'll catch him, and if he's not a snitch, he won't."

Josiah glared. "I have no idea what you're talking about, do you?"

"No, I don't, but using Clete as a diversion, we can free Kat and Millie's families and the girls. Trust me."

My cousin snickered then busted out laughing. "You have no clue right now, do you? You're rambling and making this crap up as you go." He rolled over onto his side and pulled a blanket over his head.

I fell asleep thinking about the Sabine River, my father's maps with the dots, yearning to speak Spanish, and wondering if Cletus was a snitch or not.

The sun ascended the Eastern sky as Josiah's brother snuck into the room through the same open window that I had crawled in and out earlier that evening.

"Welcome, Robert. Where did you sneak off to last night?" Cousin Cletus asked then plopped on the floor.

"I've been meaning to ask you the same questions. I haven't seen you here except for dinner last night. The last time I was home, I talked to my pa. He told me you and him were having some talks."

"Yeah, something you might be interested in, too. By the way, when you go to the caves, you need to be more discreet. Saw you going down there. I was hiding out when you climbed in. Bet you didn't know that, did ya?"

"Why didn't you say something?"

"In my line of work, I can't trust a soul, especially with rumors circling through the winds of the bayous by your pa's place saying you're gonna need my help."

I rushed towards my cousin, pulled him up by his collar. He smelled like the swamp. "Watcha know about it?"

"It's the wind howling, but the wind howling means different things in the bayou than over here in plantation life. Winds over there means spirits are acting up. The winds over here mean an escape is happening." He scooted to his bed and sat on the edge. He scrunched his face, his blue eyes boring into mine. "The winds kept howling the same song. You two are cooking up something, aren't ya? You are gonna need me."

I glanced at Josiah, who was now sitting up on his bed. He peeked at me, then his brother. "Clete, the trees don't talk to us. It's the wind blowing."

"Big brother, you are talking like Pa. The slaves know what's up. I was talking to the Johnsons last night about being the new servants inside to replace Robert's slave girlfriend." He looked straight at me, his face still wound like a ball of rubber bands. I couldn't tell when he was going to bounce off a wall. The kid could antagonize. "Why are you sneaking in their place, anyway?"

My pa wasn't a gambler, but I prayed I inherited his stoic poker face. I stared at my younger cousin, refusing to answer. So far, Cletus had already spotted me in the caves west of my father's place and now in Kat's family's quarters. This kid was like a fox or an oracle. They warned me about him. Did his father put him on my trail? Was his father some misinformed prophet? How can I use him to my advantage? I knew the answer and would not share it but with one person. When I figured out the rest, only Kat would know.

I didn't say nothing to him or Josiah. I wanted Josiah to check on the ledgers, sell the Johnsons off. He was the business manager, and I was the trainee. Zeke wasn't the brightest, but we could not underestimate him. The overseer kept a watch on the shenanigans in the fields but lacked knowledge on the day-to-day operations. Josiah and I already fudged the books. I needed to go over them with him, no matter who was watching.

I planned on riding the morning away, teaching my older cousin to ride like the wind, befriend the Caddo whom we might need. After the ride, we would arrange the sale even though I disdained when all slaves got sold. The family next to Kat's was a recent purchase and strategically placed in the same shanty with just a separate room. Josiah could place them for sale and Uncle Zeke wouldn't know.

We took off in the morning, riding southwest towards the Caddo reservation. We crossed the savannah grasses and zigzagged through the pecans prevalent in the area. I didn't think Josiah stood a chance against me. My horse was quicker than his, and I considered his equestrian style more meticulous than mine. I grabbed the lead one hundred yards in through the grassland, aware when we approached the bayous, swamps and forests, he slowed down. I continued at a slower pace.

This morning's run was a practice. I needed to see exactly what he could do. I waited fifteen minutes for him to become more confident in his riding. Josiah had to do it on his own, since we might have to split up. Plus, practice makes perfect.

Josiah arrived at our midway point, where we would turn around. It was a few hundred yards shy of the Caddo mounds. However, young tribesmen frequented the area, hunting, trapping, and gathering food for their people.

"Robert Barnum, what are you doing?" the elder of the young braves asked.

"I'm waiting for Josiah. My cousin needs to work on his speed. I want him to ride like me. Anything you guys can teach him?" I already knew the answer.

"Master Barnum, I want to watch him ride. He might not be in the proper position. Is he bent over far enough? Does he lean into the turns all the way? He might lack the confidence to sprint. You said he should arrive soon. Let me watch him gallop, see how he sits. After a break, let's ride across the field and cut through the bayou. I will ride next to him. Once again you lead, let us chase you, while I will check his riding position." He tapped his deerskin moccasin covered foot, impatiently waiting for my cousin. "Are you that much faster?"

I reckoned I was, but no one, not even the quickest of the Caddo, could match me. I tapped my feet with him to an unknown song I heard in Kat's cabin. "He should be here unless something happened. He needs to pick up the speed. We'll be galloping out of here soon."

"Robert, sometimes you must ride with caution, especially if the rumors I hear are true about why you might be leaving."

I interrupted. "What rumors?"

"Rumors I heard from your younger cousin. Master Cletus."

I looked at the young Native man. "Let's go."

We both mounted our steeds and headed off to the bayou. I wondered how much Cletus knew about what we were planning. I didn't trust him but wondered if Josiah did.

We crossed the clearing and waited at the forest edge. There was only one main trail, so it was unlikely Josiah got lost. Josiah soon rode through the clearing. On spotting us, he yanked the reins to halt the horse and dismounted. His breathing was heavy.

"Clete was there, so I had to come up with something. I struggled to come up with a reason I'd be riding through here. Told him we were racing and as always, you were beating me. He asked me why we were racing through here, and if we got something going on by the river?"

"Josiah, he knows. He ain't no dummy. He saw me in the caves, in Kat's cabin, and he intercepted you. Don't tell him anything."

"Remember, he's calculating. I never told but I know he's on our side. He helps runaways. It's what he does."

"Josiah, I heard he works on both sides. He knows conductors and catchers in Texas. I'm not sure what the criteria are for freedom or capture."

He called my bluff. I had no proof either way. All I knew was I couldn't trust the youngest brother further than I could toss him.

"Robert, as far as I know, he don't know no catchers. He created them tunnels by your pa's place. I know that for a fact, and he uses them."

The native boy looked at us as if he had something to add to the conversation. He stuttered. "I've seen him with slave girls crossing through our territory. He never takes a group, only one maiden. I've also seen him return with them and sometimes by himself. He might give the girls some sort of ritual. Maybe he takes them there to make them women and has no plan to help them."

I looked at him with widened yes, questioning his statement. "So, if they refuse, he sends them on their way to possible freedom, but has them rounded up? If they accept, then he returns to arrange an escape."

"I know nothing about that. All I have seen is that he rides like you through the reservation with young negress women and returns alone or with the girl."

We looked at Josiah. His eyes ricocheted between the two of us. He removed his hat and placed it back on his head before he spoke. "All I know is he's a sneak and mentioned to me that he could help me get Millie out of there. He knows we've been doing it off and on, and I confessed my love to her. I trust him, but not totally. I agree we can use him, but only so much."

"Perfect," I told him. "That's exactly what we need." I said nothing more since I was still figuring this out.

Josiah was ready to ride back after his horse fed and drank from the stream. I needed the Brave to watch him ride, so I asked Josiah to sprint around the clearing. He had to improve his skills if we were to be a success. I needed to work on my intelligence and leadership. We needed to be unstoppable.

I led the way. "Catch me," I hollered, as my horse and I sprinted across the field then I leaned, forcing the horse to turn.

I rode still leaned over the horse's neck, only losing a bit of speed. In the next straight away we galloped towards where I'd turn. Josiah never made-up ground lost a bit until we reached the stopping point. The Indian boy, about our age, kept a careful eye on him.

"He rides too straight in the saddle. He must lean over further in the turns, plus he must ride lower, as well as crouch lower. Confidence is what he needs, and that comes with practice. Do you want to tell him or should I?"

"I'll tell him on the way. We must get moving. He's going to help me with the books."

Josiah rode up as we finished talking. I knew he should have been closer. This would require time to get him up to my speed, and I still wanted to push it faster. It doesn't matter how fast you ride, there will always be someone quicker in the saddle, especially when carrying another body and a saddlebag.

We waved to our friend, possibly to never see him again, and rode back through the forest. We rode easy at first so we could talk.

I initiated the conversation in between trotting through thick groves of pecan trees. "John told me that you need to move with the horse. Lean further into the turn, crouch over him more. We must practice daily on this route and to the river."

"Hell, Robert, I'll be able to pass you. I don't need the practice. I know what I can do when I must, and I ride just fine." He kicked his steed and took off.

I waited a minute watching him, but my horse carried a competitive flare which I didn't have and took off. I held tight as we cut through the trees, chasing my older cousin, and caught him by the beginning of the clearing. We trotted across the clearing.

"Not bad." I smiled at him as we finished.

Chapter 4

After lunch, we buried our faces into Uncle Zeke's books. Our goal was simple; arrange a sale of the Johnsons, the new servants. Simple ledger entries were all it should take. Josiah skimmed through the books.

"Robert, look at this!"

"What is it?" I came by the desk and glanced at the paper.

He grabbed the feather leaf pen and pointed to the sales area he was going to scribble in the Johnsons. I looked it over in shock. There were no names, just a cabin number. Zeke never addressed the field slaves by name and not human in his eyes. Occasionally, the servants were called by name. Field slaves only by cabin.

I grabbed the ledger and scanned it over. I pointed to the marking in the book and said nothing. Uncle Zeke must be around.

We walked to the edge of the room, and he whispered to me. "They're selling Kat next week. My pa is taking her to New Orleans." He turned the ledger to the following days. "The rest of the family is being auctioned off here the next week."

"We have to get her before then." I wanted to shout, but there were big ears around the place. "I need to get back to my pa's and get a map with the dots." I headed for the door to ride back. Uncle Zeke stopped me.

"Where you going, boy?" He stood tall, fiddling with his suspenders, a cigar hanging from his lips.

"I was going home. I think my pa needs me for something."

"My brother doesn't need no help. I need you here to keep those no-good slaves of mine in line. I might have to fire that drunk overseer. Clete been catching him wandering down by the cabins. I'm afraid he might fraternize with the women. I'm gonna fire his drunk ass, and I need someone to take his place. You crack that whip like no one I've seen. Next time don't miss."

I soon became overseer of Uncle Zeke's plantation. A job I never saw coming but could use to my advantage. I wondered how much Uncle Zeke knew. Did he have an informant? Was it Cletus or Josiah? Was it the servants? Did they know anything? Could my uncle be smarter than I thought? We had to act fast, since I was ready to take her tonight.

He led me into the office where Josiah crunched the numbers. Josiah looked up as I entered the room. We couldn't speak about details since his father escorted me.

"Josiah, Robert, sit down, I need to speak with you, "my uncle said as he sat behind his mahogany desk. He stifled his cigar in the ashtray, twirling smoke around.

Josiah and I sat across from him.

He continued, "I'm changing the plantation. I had to fire overseer Jenkins. Rumors had it he was fraternizing with the slaves. I'm also selling off some of the trouble making slaves. Cabin 7." He paused, trying to remember the correct cabin number.

Josiah grabbed the ledger again. He handed him the book, not wanting to glance at the change he made.

"7b. There are rumors about them fraternizing with the family." He stared me down. "I have moved the girl and her mother from the house, and now plan on selling the former servant. I've planned to take her to New Orleans for the next auction. Josiah, I want you to take Robert to his new quarters."

I kept silent. I could have been at the saloon in town, playing poker. No one could read my face as thoughts of the escape raced through my mind as fast as my horse could ride.

Once we were out of sight from his father, I turned to my cousin. "Did Clete set this up?"

Josiah walked along, smiled and shook his head. His smile got bigger, however he said nothing. He was the brains of the operation. I walked into my new home, a small cabin, slightly bigger than the slaves cabin built for two families. I'd live alone and wondered how slaves lived their daily routine.

We walked in and the place reeked of alcohol. Jenkins was an alcoholic. It might have been the reason Uncle Zeke fired him. I looked back at my cousin. He wore a smirk. I sat on the edge of the cot. He came up next to me and looked around. Zeke did not follow us.

"I dumped a bottle of whiskey in here. I switched the sale to the Johnsons and recommended you for the overseer. It gives you a great opportunity to work with all of father's help, especially Kat and Millie, including their families to get them out of here. We still need to roll this week. My father isn't as dumb as we think, and we can't trust him."

"What about your brother?"

"Let's watch him. I'm setting him up as well."

"Okay, I have access to Kat and Millie, so you can get Clete to set up the diversion."

"We must be across the river when the diversion happens. We're not sacrificing the girls' families for our escape. I'd rather they go in peace, and we're taking the risk. Clete will inadvertently lead them in our direction when the families take off. We need to be across the river or buried in a cave."

"I know the caves, but so does he. Do you think he'll lead them toward the burrows?"

"How many are there?"

"Several, plus hollowed cypress trees. We need at least a day to get hidden and buried." I informed him.

"I know he won't tattle, at least not at first, and by that time we should be long gone."

"How do you know he won't say anything?"

Josiah lowered his voice to a whisper. "He'll have to explain. Remember, he's been doing this as well. Pa would kill him if he found out."

I pondered over my brain trust's strategy and pounded him with questions. "How are we going to keep him from finding out we left?"

"I can't tell you."

"Why not?"

"I haven't figured it out. I got us this far."

"Do you want me to pick a date and go? I need to get supplies from my fathers and say goodbye."

"Look at your quarters here. Nothing in them. Now head to your father's and get back in the morning. I got this from here."

My steed loved night jaunts. He knew the route by heart so easily he galloped through Caddo land towards Pa's shanty until we arrived in the middle of the night at about two in the morning. I snuck into Pa's office in search of the maps of East Texas to seek out the green dots peppered on the map. I planned on getting some shuteye before leaving, but also plotted grabbing some rope, knives, shovels and a rifle. The clicking of a revolver made my heart skip. I almost jumped from my skin. I spun to the sound of the pistol to see the barrel flashing in the candlelight. On recognizing me, Father replaced the gun in his holster. I heard him sigh in relief.

"Son, what are you doing here? You're supposed to be at my brothers."

"Two things, Father. I need the maps, and I have to say goodbye. We're leaving this week."

"Are you sure? Do you have everything worked out?

"Nope, Zeke plans on taking Kat to New Orleans for the auction. Josiah made some changes in the ledger, but Zeke ain't that stupid. We must get her out this week. Josiah arranged it to have Jenkins fired and for me to become the new overseer."

My father pondered my statement. He removed his spectacles and stovetop hat, scratched his head, and returned them to position. "This will give you access to them, and one less person watching. It should free you up. Josiah thought of this?"

"He didn't tell me, but I could tell since he had that smirk on his face. I knew he did it."

Father got his map of East Texas out, and I studied them again. The first stop was a two-day ride near Jasper, headed straight for the border. We'd be riding at night, hiding in the day, searching for the lit candle in the window once we arrived at Jasper.

"Son, these aren't exact. However, they are close. We can't pinpoint the exact locations of the farms but look for the candle in the window. It's universal. Another thing is that I admire you for doing this, I wish it was for the honor of all and not just your personal desire, but if you have the calling to free this girl, and make a life together, may your family be blessed. I will say you a prayer before bed, in case I don't see you in the morning. Let me quote you Joshua1.5 NO MAN

43

SHALL BE ABLE TO STAND BEFORE YOU ALL THE DAYS OF YOUR LIFE. JUST AS I WAS WITH MOSES, SO I WILL BE WITH YOU. I WILL NOT LEAVE YOU OR FORSAKE YOU."

I read along in silence, knowing God would be on our side. I packed up a bedroll, then slept in my father's place for the last time that evening. We'd be passing by one more time and possibly sleeping in the caves near the river. I planned to head back to Zeke's early morning. Before departing, my father and I said our goodbyes in tears. I promised to write him from Mexico.

The next morning, I woke before my father, mounted my horse and brushed the tears away. With one final glance at my pa's house, I rode back to my uncles.

I arrived shortly before lunch and noticed two shadows standing at the entrance. One was tall and gangly, and the other appeared fatter. Trotting closer, I made out Josiah and his father, who held a bull whip, which he started cracking as I approached the duo.

"Where were ya, boy?" Zeke shouted.

"I rode out to my fathers to get some clothes, blanket, bible and a few other possessions." I had the map already wadded up and hidden in a pocket, aware he'd search my belongings.

"Give me the stuff. I'll have the Johnsons make up your bed, but there was no reason to leave, especially without my permission."

"Sorry, sir. I needed some supplies if I'm living here." Of course, I lied, but I preferred my own Bible and blanket to theirs. Zeke marked those special verses defending his evil practice.

"Cabin 7 was late for their chores. There was no overseer, so they were late. You need to discipline them. Ride off and bring them here. I'll show ya how to whip them, then you'll do it. I need to train you, my way." He grabbed my arm and shoved me forward.

I stumbled over a pecan tree root and fell on my face. I stayed down, reining in my temper before attempting to rise, only to be shoved to the ground by my uncle. I fell flat on my face. The whip snapped at my back, sending blinding pain through my body. "Run off again or disobey the training. You'll get it like dem niggers. Understand, boy?" He snapped the whip again, this time missing by inches.

I looked at Josiah, who appeared to grimace. His face had a stifled protest; his mouth hung wide open.

"What are you looking at? Go round them up and bring them to me, boy. Now!"

Again, the whip snapped at my feet. He either missed or aimed at the ground. I got on my horse and rode off, but not before my uncle handed me his whip. "They should be at the orchard harvesting pecans. Now get out and bring them to the house in twenty minutes. Don't be afraid to whip them if they don't come."

I galloped towards the orchard behind the slave quarters at the east end of the plantation. Last I knew; they were the only family harvesting the nuts. I needed to talk with Kat's family in private. I kicked my steed, forcing the horse into a mild gallop.

The orchard was the furthest from my escape route, however it ventured onto the southern end into a clearing from which I could increase my speed toward the reservation, then the river. I saw Kat and the other ladies kneeling with gunny sacks, examining the nuts before tossing them inside the bag. The men climbed the trees to shake them out. Kat noticed me and her smile lit up the orchard. She sprinted to me.

"Master Barnum, you coming to rescue us?" she screamed louder than she should have.

I placed my finger on my lips, dismounted and whispered, "Not yet, but soon." As overseer, I embraced my role. "I need to take you back to the house. Master Zeke needs you. Gentlemen, please, come down now."

One of her older brothers hesitated. The other men climbed down from the trees.

"C'mon sir." I wanted to treat them with respect, something they never received from Overseer Jenkins. "I'm the new overseer, and I don't want to use this." As a varmint slipped away wounded, I snapped the whip toward it.

"You are on our side," he shouted down at me.

"I need to do this." I insisted. "I need to play this up to make everything work out."

"You ain't gonna be no cracker, are ya?"

"I gotta do what I must do. I hope I don't have to, but for everything to go as I'm planning, I might have to. Now c'mon down, because I can get you from the ground."

He sat in the tree about twenty feet off the ground, near the middle. The whip I carried was longer than that, and I was an expert. I could knock a nut out of the tree, and I decided to nail a branch with unharvested pecans where he stood.

The nuts dropped to the ground, and I snapped back the whip. Kat's sibling began scaling down the tree. Kat rushed to harvest the pecans. She inspected them and stuffed them in the gunny.

"Mastah Barnum, you trying to whoop me?" he screamed, taking a few steps forward to get in my face. His family stopped him.

At first, I glanced at Kat, then approached her father.

"Sir, you know I don't wanna do this, but it will open room for us. I'm sure I can get you out ahead of me. Then we'll ride the opposite way. It's going to go down in the next couple of nights. Play Pompey Ran Away, have things packed, I can get you on a riverboat that is headed north, while we'll ride South to Mexico. For now, sir, we must go along to earn Master's trust. He's gonna make me whoop ya, and you know I don't like that."

We strolled back to the house with me on horseback following the family from cabin 7a. Uncle Zeke and Josiah stood waiting.

"Get them over here and gimme that whip boy. I need to teach these niggers a lesson. Get the girl, first. Robert, strip her down."

I ripped off her dress, but not tearing it, since she had limited clothing. Her top was now worn below her waist. Zeke ripped the whip from my hands, burning my palm with the velocity he tore it from me. My hands shook, and I grimaced from the sting of the burn. Kat glanced at me. I despised seeing her this way and wanted to make the getaway now. She took seven shots to the back and never cried, while I stood helpless. Then he handed me the whip. It was my turn for the next five. Her gigantic eyes pleaded with me to go easy on her. I didn't know how to crack one easy, and only knew one way to miss. My uncle knew the only way to miss was intentionally. I took one step closer and rolled the bullwhip, my wrist cocked. I snapped my wrist forward five straight times. I hit the same spot every time and broke the skin. She'd have a scar, hopefully not for life, but damaged by what I did.

She glared at me. I refused to look at the pain in her eyes. This wouldn't last more than a day. I'd have time with them and with Millie's family in a short time. First things first were gaining Zeke's trust. We moved to the family members. There would be seven more, including Kat's youngest siblings, about seven and eight years old. Whipping the youngsters was as painful as smacking the switch on Kat, maybe more. Once finished, I escorted them back to their quarters.

"Tomorrow night we're doing this, so tonight can be a test. Play the songs on the banjo when you hear me riding up for inspection. I'll nab Kat and ride to the bayou. Stay put, and I'll return to see if I can pull this off. Right now, I need to study the maps."

The family ventured back to the orchard. Kat stopped and turned towards me. "Robert, are we going to do this?"

"Yes, it will be dangerous. We could die if we're caught. Are you sure you want to go?"

"With you, yes. I know you can do it. Besides, I'd rather be dead than work in the orchard and get whooped because I gave you an extra piece of chicken, and today we were only ten minutes late."

"You know I don't want to whip ya, your family, or anyone."

"I know." She peered up at me with those big brown eyes. "You're planning our future and did what you have to do. You're also a slave to him."

"That's ending soon," I told her as we walked toward the orchard." I need to get with Mildred. Where are they at?"

"They should also be in the orchard." She pointed to a grove of trees.

I made out some bodies as we continued our stroll. "Should we head over?"

I peeked around in search of any other hired hands but didn't see anyone. I aided Kat upon my horse. She sat there proudly, a smile brightening her sad face. Then she glanced down. I was ready to ride now, but I needed to plan tonight. I led the horse into the grove, letting Kat hold the reins. We found Millie's family but didn't spot her right away.

· "She's up there in the trees," Kat said.

"Millie, c'mon down, right now." I practiced my authoritative voice.

She climbed down the tree and jumped into the savannah with a tumble.

We led her away from her family and the other slaves towards a brief clearing deeper into the forest. I glanced around, making mental notes of the details of the land. Josiah knew it better, same reason I allowed him to take the lead in routing us out of there. He was smarter than me.

"We're getting you out of here in one of the next two nights. Rumors are Master Barnum might take you or Kat to New Orleans for the auction. We want to get you to Mexico to be our brides."

"Josiah told me that already. I be keeping a secret too. When we going?"

"What about your family?"

"Josiah working on a plan for them with Kat's. According to Josiah, they can't catch all of them."

"Master or some catcher down the road might kill them. We don't want that."

Millie pointed towards the orchards. "Look up there. My family shakes nuts from trees for food and a small hut to live in. Mastah Barnum makes all the money, and we do all the work. That's what my daddy says."

I got the diversion I needed. The pecan orchards would work perfect.

Chapter 5

I returned to the overseer's cabin, my temporary home and found Josiah pacing the floor, back and forth across the wood. Fury shot out from his eyes like daggers.

"Robert, we gotta act tonight. Pop is selling Kat and Millie tomorrow. He is taking them to Narleans first thing, before the bullfrogs' croak. Seems like he needs the money and need to cut back. Getting rid of the troublemakers."

"He is only selling those two?" I pulled up a chair and spun it around before sitting.

"I saw the books. They've changed since I changed them." He held up a ripped page from his father's ledger. "Glad I kept an eye on things. Father and Cletus are taking them."

"Cletus is a snitch."

"Maybe."

"We need to use him on a diversion." I scratched my chin.

"I told Kat and her father that we're going for a test tonight. Let Clete know we gotta sacrifice someone."

"Who are we sacrificing? We can't do the future in-laws."

"The squealers? The Johnson's."

"How we gonna set Clete and them up?"

"You're the brains. You tell me."

Josiah bent his head over, forehead resting on his fist. He mumbled, not in prayer. He was in thought, jiggling ideas around in his head. He looked at me.

"I'll talk to him. I'm sure that Ol' Man Johnson dug some dirt up on Pops. He gotta escape. Clete's helping him get to the river east so that they can hide out on a riverboat. I got actual schedules. Once they be gone for a half hour and father's men head east, we head west towards the river. Not sure yet about Millie and Kat's kin. They might hide out with the Caddo or your pappy. Maybe the tunnels."

"Those are Clete's tunnels, remember?"

"Exactly. That is the frame up right there. We need your pa's help for the families. Get the right boat up the Sabine. They got one of those yellow lights on the Texas side of Logansport. I know everything Clete knows, but he don't know everything I know. Damn, little brothers need taught a lesson."

"We need to skedaddle first. Clete will help the Johnsons. I'll set a trap. They won't make five miles."

I took off east into the night. I went past Uncle's land and further into a neighboring plantation where resided Zeke's nemesis, a man whose land was twice the size of my uncles and often mocked my kinfolk for owning a fraction of the land he had. Crossing it safe without a trap would be difficult. Diversions and sacrifices were required. I stole one of Uncle's kerosene lanterns and placed it three miles into his neighbor's pecan grove, near the clearing where one could see the house. Josiah would tell his brother where the marker would be. If the plan went on without a hitch, it would give Kat and Millie's families time to get to the tunnels, where my father could help. I needed one more player. The young Native man, who was supposed to teach Josiah to ride. He'd accompany our girl's families in a wagon, while they laid in the back covered in pecan nuts, cotton, and whatever else we could scoop over them.

I rode back and did a quick bed check. The plan was working. Cletus was speaking with the Johnsons as I checked each one. I stopped at the end and gave Millie the signal. She peeked at me, smiling. Her father handed me his gourd banjo that sat next to the wood-burning stove. I attempted to play Pompey Ran Away but couldn't play like Kat's pa, but Millie's dad raised his eyebrows, while a slight grin surfaced on his face, as he bent his head in prayer, and acknowledged what was happening as we peeked out the door to Kat's cabin. He shut the door as I snuck up to Kat's shanty. I didn't hear Cletus anymore except rumbling in the Johnson's cabin. I barged for an unannounced bed check.

"Making sure no has snuck out," I told Mr. Johnson. "Is the family all here?" I shone the light around the room. The youngest daughter was not there. She was probably off with Clete or Uncle Zeke. I paid it no mind.

"We'se all here. We ain't going nowhere," the father said. I knew he was lying, but again, I didn't care. The attempted escape was needed.

"I'm just checking, doing the job Master Zeke pays me to do. See ya folks in the house for breakfast." I tipped my cap and snuck next door.

A quiet squeal shocked my ear when Kat saw me. She looked eager to flee.

I turned to her father. "Tonight, we ride. Wait an hour after The Johnsons go. They won't make it far. Play that song, so Millie's family will be ready to roll. You should be able to walk to the edge of the land through the forest. Our Caddo brothers will wait for you. I got one more detail to prepare, and we're running for freedom."

My next stop was The Caddo. I needed them but they didn't know it. We galloped across the land, skirting west, slashing through the bayous, forests, and savannahs. I wanted to think I did it in record time. Next time I headed this direction, it would be faster, even with the extra weight. My pony would need to be well fed and rested. Right now, he was getting a workout. Once I hit the edge of their territory, I trotted up. My friend, John, greeted me.

"Robert, what are you doing here at this hour?"

"I need you, that's what I'm doing. You and one of your bravest brothers. I need two wagons full of produce. Follow me to the edge of Zeke's land. You will know what to do when you see them. Josiah and I will either be in the tunnels or across the river. Go get them wagons. If they're empty, fill them half-way. We'll be trotting back, and this steed needs a break."

I stopped at the creek so my horse could plop his snout in the creek to lap up some water. I fed him some berries I picked earlier. The horse worked hard tonight and will push himself later.

My Caddo brother followed as I headed back. They knew the route; they knew what to do. I trusted them. Once close enough, I made a dash across Uncle's land and hitched my horse. Josiah's pony stood patient and ready, tied to the post. I snuck in my shanty, where Josiah waited. His saddlebag sat stuffed and overflowing while his possessions sat on the table. He looked all set to ride.

"I'm ready to go." His boots left marks on the mud floor as he paced my quarters. His eyes shone through the flickering light.

"We need to rest a bit. We can't be tired, especially if we're crossing the Sabine. I've been riding back and forth nonstop. It also tuckered the pony out. I need a little shuteye," I told him, stretching out on my cot.

My cousin twirled the lone chair in my shack around and straddled it. "Clete might be on to it. The little shit is clever, but then that Johnson girl is his weakness. I caught him giving it to her in the barn. I told him he can give it to her all he wants in Canada. He smiled at me, but it was his other smile, the one he showed us before Pa changed things around."

"One hour then." I pulled my hat over my eyes since I needed rest.

My cousin woke me two hours later. "You said I'm the brains. It's time."

I checked my pocket watch through the illumination the kerosene lantern provided. It wasn't quite midnight.

"Let's do it," I told him, extinguishing the lamp.

We calmed the horses so they wouldn't neigh and walked the beasts across the land towards their quarters until it was safe to mount. I dismounted, snuck in to get Kat, and aided her on the horse. I grabbed her father's musical squash and we hit Millie's cabin. Josiah followed. In the euphoria of this tiny victory, I played a little ditty on the three stringed vegetable, while Kat crooned the lyrics,

"I looked over the Jordan and what did I see,

Coming for to carry me home.

There was a band of angels, a-coming after me,

Coming for to carry me home."

Millie knew what was up. She smiled at us and dashed through the door to kiss my cousin, passing the banjo back to her father. All set to go, she hugged her family goodbye. Over her shoulders, she spoke to her friend, "I'll sing you the next verse if we get split up."

Josiah assisted her on his animal.

My cousin and I both gouged our animals in the kidneys without spurs. Our girls gripped our stomachs as we disappeared into the forest. We cut in and out between the pecan trees that made up the orchard. Josiah remained hot on my trail close behind. We met the Caddo near the clearing; I slowed enough to tip my hat as we galloped across the clearing towards their land. Kat gripped me tighter as we trotted through the mounds, skipping past domed shaped homes that I didn't notice because of the dark, star-filled sky.

All this time, Josiah stayed on my trail. He didn't lose too much ground on me. Either his horse was fresh compared to mine that was, or my cousin might have picked up his pace a bit. We wove through the Caddo territory reducing our speed, rested our horses a dab, then dashed through the tall trees and bayous, separating Caddo land from my father's. It stretched about ten miles as groves of Pecans turned into Cypress trees, which we barely made out. It took about an hour to navigate the swamps. We had been riding about four hours and needed a rest, but Pa's place was about five miles away. The Sabine might be another mile. Pa had a barn, where we could hide the horses if needed, while we hid in the caves and burrows until it was safe.

Once we cleared the swamp, I let Josiah catch up. We recollected our thoughts, let our racing hearts even up the beating and allowed the steed to catch a quick breath. One last sprint to my father's house, then I waited for my cousin. Once he finished his rest, we galloped across the tall Savanna grass at top speed and approached the barn that sat behind Pa's.

"Take them inside Pa's house. We should be good for tonight. Zeke ain't gonna know what hit him until morning."

"Pa ain't that stupid, plus we don't know which side Clete is working. The Johnsons might not have even attempted. This is the first place they'll look. We need to assume he's on our trail. My father will have hunters out searching here. The best bet is to get to a cave. Remember, Robert, if stealing Pa's property went without a hitch, there wouldn't be no slaves in this part of Louisiana."

I took off my hat, wiped my hand through my long hair, and used the time to ponder over his statement. "I want to hit the caves when there is some sunlight. We both know who lives in there. Reptiles, some are bigger than the house, Also, venomous snakes, and none like woken up. I want to get down there and make room for us. It was an idea I had before we rushed off."

"Uncle Jeremiah don't have no place to hide us."

"Oh yes, he does. We've got hidden walls. Not a lot of room, but enough for three. I'll be in the caves. Our best bet is to wait a couple of days. The sheriff and catchers will expect us to ride like the wind. We need to keep them off guard as much as possible."

"I agree. We don't know what lay ahead of us. This will be the first place they look, but not the last. They might have dogs sniffing out the trail, but they'd be sniffing the quick route."

"Yeah, we took a little longer, cut through more trees. If the hounds don't pick up any of our scents, they might search other directions, which will give us a few more days."

I succeeded in calming the horses, fed and roped them up in the back of Pa's barn. The girls huddled close to me and my cousin, each one in our arms.

"We ain't free yet. Are we?" Kat asked me.

"We might never be free. It's best we die trying than living as property and be damned sure I ain't gonna enforce it. Master Zeke might be up and about now. His plan is to take both of you to Narleans and auction you girls off. That's why we rode tonight."

Kat wore a blank look, still shocked at what had happened. Not over four hours ago, she slept on a mud floor with her siblings and parents. Now she was separated from her family; their whereabouts would remain unknown. It hit me she had no say in the ordeal, as Josiah and I continued on treating her like property.

Chapter 6

Ezekiel and Cletus Barnum.

Cletus Barnum, youngest of the three cousins, as well as the least trusted, entered his father's bedroom. The stars shone bright as the Louisiana moon descended. The candle flickered by the window as Cletus's father snored, anticipating the day he'd take the two harlots to New Orleans for auction. Cletus was coming with and the youngest needed his initiation into manhood. Two willing or unwilling slaves headed for auction would suit him just fine. Little did the master of the plantation know that his youngest had no concern or issues with the young African descendants.

"Papa." The boy screamed loud enough to wake the roosters into cawing. "They gone. They gone. Kat and Mildred both be gone. So are Josiah and Robert."

His father tossed on some overalls, lit a kerosene lantern, and marched across the dark acreage with his youngest son on his heels. They made it halfway across the plantation, a hundred yards away, before a group of four Negroes bust from the lead cabin. It was the Johnsons.

"Go get em, boy," he yelled to his son.

"I'm gonna let them run. We can catch them darkies later. They are a decoy for Kat and Millie. Robert and Josiah set this up."

"You defying me, boy?" His father screamed as the Johnsons crept further into the forest. "Bring down two horses and let's skedaddle over to capture them no good house niggers. Then we'll round up your brother and cousin. They all gonna get what they deserve." Zeke fiddled for his pistol.

Through the night sky, Cletus saw his father's glowing eyes, even the pulsating veins in his neck. There were times he could outsmart his father, but there were others he had best obey. Cletus Barnum didn't always know the difference. That morning, he listened.

Cletus brought out both horses, his and his father's. They rode east towards the brightening skies. "Son, watcha know about this?" the old man asked. He had calmed down a bit though they continued to gallop through groves of pecan trees.

Zeke carried a torch in one hand, the other gripping the reins. He tried to gauge him through the flicker of light, with the intent to betray his brother and cousin. After all, it was the beautiful Kat he wanted to run away with. The way her dark skin glowed in the moonlight, the stars reflecting in her eyes, he had hoped to glimpse her bathing. Whether he wanted honest relations with her or to use her as the others he aided in escaping, he wasn't sure.

"It was Robert all along. He tried to lure me. He used me as a decoy. Josiah let him look at the books. He must have noticed the sale and decided to escape tonight. I'm not sure how you trusted him as overseer."

"We'll catch him. I don't care if he's my weak brother's son. He's getting a noose when we catch him. Now, for your brother, I don't know what we gonna do with him. I didn't raise him that way. I knew him and that girl had been doing it but didn't think he could love a nigra." He lifted the reins, stifling the horse. Clete followed suit. "Now, to answer your question. Why did you recommend Robert? You said you wanted to keep it in the family."

Cletus gazed at the fallen nuts on the path. He raised his eyes to his father. "Pa, I didn't. You chose him. It's a job I wanted." A tear fell.

"Boy, we're losing time. Go fetch them, Johnsons. I'm not sure why they wanted to run. I treated them good."

He hesitated to take off. Ezekiel Barnum was sure the boy was up to something. The boy galloped off while the father spun around determined to put a price on his nephew's head.

Zeke stopped at the plantation. He proceeded to arm himself in preparation to head north to the village nearest the plantation. He rounded up a posse, ordering them to kill Robert, brand his son a thief. For Kat and Millie, he had more disgusting plans for them. Through the shadows of a rising sun, raping the girls wouldn't be good enough. The pastor lit up a cigar, his lips and eyes crunched together. He whipped his horse, urging the animal to gallop towards the parish sheriff.

"Lyle, gather a posse up. That little, no-good nephew of mine stole a couple of my young Negresses. Rode straight off. They are probably at that no-good trouble making little brother of mine." Zeke shouted from atop his horse, still approaching Lyle Thibodaux's office. "Round up the village. We gonna get him and put up some posters. Little shit ain't stealing my property from under my nose."

Zeke led the men that the posse rounded up across the fields, where they spotted a young, brave dressed in traditional gathering dress, roaming bareback on his horse. The lad carried a rifle in the hope to shoot some game. He spotted the posse and dismounted. He guessed why they were coming and who they were chasing. Their target passed through hours earlier, but he didn't know the itinerary. Even if he did, he wasn't telling.

Zeke galloped up to the brave shouting. "You see Josiah and his cousin? Did they pass through here?"

The young lad said nothing.

"Ezekiel," Sheriff Thibodaux called. "Dat injun got a gun. He looks ornery as hell, too." The sheriff didn't think twice. Though the Caddo were peaceful, the young man had a rifle. Zeke and the sheriff didn't care if the kid only used the gun for nailing a deer. They could say he attacked, and it was self-defense. He was the sheriff, after all. The kid took a bullet through his heart and splatting into the mud. His body left an impression in the dirt as the posse moved on.

They galloped through the reservation, not worried about being followed. The destination was Zeke's brother's small cabin. His younger brother, also smaller and more of a pacifist, wouldn't know what hit him when confronted with being a wanted man for harboring slaves. Zeke knew his brother was an abolitionist and possibly aided the escape of the slaves. If found guilty, Zeke had no issue with locking his brother up. Hanging his kin was still an option, if forced to. Lynching his brother's only child wasn't an option, but destiny.

The posse scurried through the reservation and soon came upon Robert's father's cabin. The place appeared vacant except for the Quaker outside working the land. Jeremiah glanced up at the sound of thirty-two hoof prints approaching.

"Big brother, Sheriff, watcha doing out here?" he called out.

"Jeremiah, I know you're my brother, but your son stole my property. I'm asking, have you seen him pass this way?" Zeke's eyes darted all over. His focus was west of the cabin, towards the Sabine River.

The younger of the two brothers was cool as the cucumbers in his garden. "I haven't seen him since this morning, when he left for your place. He said you hired him

60

to be the new overseer and that jobs are scarce these days. Doubt if he would have run off."

"My oldest boy, your boy, and those two slave girls they be messing with are gone. Sheriff here thinks we need to search your property."

"Go ahead. No one is here. Feel free." Jeremiah led the posse to his cabin. His breathing was steady, and he showed no signs of hiding stolen property. The search party invaded the younger preacher's cabin, pillaged the shanty, tossed everything in sight, even checked for hidden walls by tapping the wood in search of a hollow sound. They found nothing.

"Let's ride off to the river. My youngest says there are caves and tunnels, including some dug-out old cypress trees. I'm sure Robert knows where they're at."

The men galloped west. Jeremiah kept it cool on the outside until the posse was out of sight. Once they vanished into the bayou, he knelt, and spoke to the one man who he listened to. God.

While he prayed to the Lord above, another young man rode up on horseback. Jeremiah's youngest nephew, Cletus Barnum, rode up far behind the search party. He never found the Johnson party because he never searched for them. His mission was to find his brother and cousin and the two escaped slaves. Unless they crossed the river, he knew where to find them. After all, in his spare time, he had dug further into the caves, creating a tunnel system for the young girls he sent west. Cletus's mission was to recover the slaves and become overseer or be assigned to run the plantation. He didn't have to ask his Uncle Jeremiah if he'd seen the fugitives. Clete knew where the hideouts were. He trotted off through the bayou, hoping he would not see the rest of the posse.

Kat and Millie's family waited in their respective cabins until Master Barnum and the posse galloped through. They stole one of Zeke's wagons and with that ventured towards Logansport in the darkness, riding at night and hiding during the day. There were safe places to hide out for a day or a week until free in The Indian Nations, north of Texas. Native Americans walked across the Southeast, being forced to live in the land between Texas and the Kansas-Nebraska territory. Some Native tribes welcomed escaped slaves; other tribes continued the tradition. This was the best option for an escape from Louisiana, unless they could sneak on a northbound Mississippi steamboat and remain hidden.

The two families crept forward in the night. So far, they were undetected. Only God knew their destination and if they would arrive safely. The fugitives hummed spirituals, singing to the God above as they crossed the Northwest Louisiana Bayous.

Chapter 7

Josiah dashed back into one of the caves. This cave was deeper into the bayou and further from the river. It was one his younger brother didn't know about. I had dug it from one of Clete's tunnels. The cavern was large enough for four people and two horses to hide for two days. It was also undetectable from the outside. Josiah entered it from an entrance that Cletus built, and he crawled through on his belly. He forced the mud through an opening and let the others know.

"They're coming," he whispered. "I heard the horses. We need to lie low."

Millie shrieked and clung to Kat, both women envisioning their premature death. I took to calming the horses as they laid on their sides. Kat and Millie rushed to me, and we sat in the dark cave in silence. Josiah crawled through and engulfed Millie in his arms.

"We're safe here. Pa and Clete don't know nothing about this one. Clete dug the others; it will be okay, dear." He kissed Millie's forehead, doing everything a preacher's kid knew how to reassure her.

I observed and learnt the best I could in the pitch-black cavern. I was new in this comforting the girl thing. Kat crawled to me, and I put my arm around her.

"Trust me, Kat, we are gonna make it out of here. Mastah will hold no claim on you, but we need to be safe. I'll sneak to my pa's once I know it's all clear and be ready to run. Right now, we need to be quiet as a mouse."

The voices got louder. I recognized Zeke but could not hear my little cousin, but also there were other voices I didn't recognize. It didn't mean Clete was with them or not. A fourteen-year old's job is to shut up and let the men talk, but he's the one I was most worried about. He's a snitch, sneaky and unpredictable. Uncle Zeke was predictable as the sun rising in the east. I didn't know the men involved, however if Zeke rounded them up, they'd be as anticipated as my uncle.

Kat buried her head in my chest. Rather than have my hands and arm hanging uselessly at my side, I put them around her, holding her tight. This wasn't a time to touch or feel her up. I held her so tight that I could feel her heart thump and her heaving breath.

"Clete, you said you've built tunnels on your uncle's property?" It came through clear as day.

I could hear them. I signaled to Josiah and the girls, hoping they could see through the shadows that the torch we set in the mud provided.

Cletus was in a dilemma. He used the tunnels to help other young women escape the plantation, but now he had to set himself up. Our eyes dashed around on each other, waiting for his response.

"Boy, I'm asking you a question. Where are these tunnels? It's daylight. We should find them with no problem."

Again silence.

Kat gripped my leg. I hoped he'd give the location of the closest ones. While digging this tunnel, I had also prepared a trap, one that my younger cousin would be proud of. They'd be easy pickings with the Beecher Bible I carried. As far as

The Sharp Rifle went, I wasn't as good as shot as Josiah, but the posse would be at close range. The bull whip was also with me.

At least Clete wasn't speaking. We couldn't tell if he was pointing out locations to the posse. Zeke was also silent, Clete must have shown them the tunnel, otherwise he would still be harking on the boy. I kept petting my horse, just like Josiah was doing. I could see our girls cling tighter and tighter to each other. No one spoke. Keeping the horses calm was the focus.

"There ain't nothing here," a member of the posse spoke.

His voice seemed to come from the cave that I added on weeks earlier. If they all crawled in and followed it to the destination, the whole posse would be two feet from us. There was a back exit, which led straight into the Sabine.

"Should we let them in?" I whispered to Josiah.

His eyes glowed in the flickering light showing an evil side I've never seen from him. "Doubt if Pa will be in. We can be in the river in two shakes of a tail and Pa won't realize what's happened until we cross."

"Okay, get the horses and the girls to the exit."

I walked him through the tunnel to point the way. He kept coaxing the ponies and ladies to follow.

"Right past here is the river. I shoveled mud, broke through to air before I crawled back.

"Still don't see nothing." Another posse member said. "You sure about these tunnels, Cletus?" the voice asked.

Finally, Cletus spoke. "Yes sheriff. Me and Robert dug this one. Robert been down here a bunch of times the last month."

I crawled to the other end to let Josiah know it's time to go. He shoved his way through the packed mud door, while I snuck back to jam the shovel through the mud. I still heard the voices as the dirt crumbled and got out the door. Josiah helped Millie on his horse. I did the same for Kat. This way, the six of us crossed the Sabine all heads bobbing under water.

Only Zeke was out as we heard him yelling. "Son, get your ass back here. You done lost everything and we are gonna find you. The rest of you are dead."

I turned around about halfway to see him pull his rifle, aim and shoot. I spotted the splash five to ten feet behind my cousin.

We crossed the hundred-foot-wide river without any more hassle, and I helped Josiah and Millie ashore. Zeke kept cursing. He waved his fist at us. I tipped my hat to him and thought I heard screams of help as we rode off on the east side, meandering through the Texas bayou.

"Which way we headed?" Josiah asked me as we all mounted the horses.

"Don't matter now. We just need to stay in the thick bayou, but we do need to move southeast," I said. "I hope we can make it to the edge of this swamp, so we can rest up and get some shut eye. Both of us will stand guard and make sure the girls stay hidden. If the posse is on our trail, they should be closing in on us by the time we're ready to head out again."

We galloped through the swamps, the cypress trees keeping us protected. We were confident that the shallow waters of the bayou hid our tracks and scents. We had two routes in mind. One was Southeast, around Jasper, there was a house on the map my father gave us with a dot, a safe haven for us. That's where the posse would expect us to go. We had to outthink the posse which shouldn't be too hard.

Straight west of us was several haven locations. A couple in Lufkin, and five in Nacogdoches. There was a spot my father marked as a possible haven, and we could make it there by the next morning. Right now, the key was to splash through this bayou with our horses galloping through the mud, and we'd push them to the limit. I chose straight west. Horror stories had been passed down and tossed around about what would happen if one traveled the most direct route. We rode the longest route to haven locations. It would take two full night rides into a land I haven't ventured into.

After pushing through the bayou, the forest began thinning out. It was time to stop for the day. The sun had passed its peak. I figured it was about one or two in the afternoon. Josiah took the girls further back in the swamp, leaving me to ride in the open, trying to figure out where in the hell I was. I searched around the quiet area that was almost too quiet for my liking. It felt like we were riding into a trap. Zeke had probably telegraphed local sheriffs and marshals about his property on the run. We'd have to be extra safe.

I rode back, after a quick scout of the surrounding land. I could see nothing suspicious. I struggled to find Kat, Josiah and Millie, which was a good thing, since they were so well-hidden near a cypress that I rode by them once. Josiah's horse whinnied at mine as I passed.

Kat ran out in the open when I approached. On seeing her, I dismounted and led the horse. My cousin set up some traps to catch a few rabbits and squirrels. He started a small fire over which we cooked the small mammals before bunking for the night. The girls hid as we shared guard duty. Each one alternating between the rest.

While the girls slept, Josiah and I kept an eye out. He questioned my leadership. "I still think we should have taken the shortest route. We'd be at a haven early in the morning."

"The posse and the law over here know it. That's what they be expecting. The more we keep them off guard the further we can ride. Your Pa ain't that bright, but he ain't stupid either. I ain't sure he even knows about the network over here."

I turned around and saw Kat. "Robert?" She came out from behind a tall cypress. "Mastah Zeke has those maps. When I was cleaning the office, I saw Cletus give him some. He's fully aware and so is your other cousin."

I looked at her, wondering if she should question my leadership. I thought about what she said and realized she supported my cockamamie plan. "Exactly, therefore we are heading this way. It should keep any posse off us. Anything else you might have discovered while cleaning?"

She looked at me with narrow eyes. Her normal big brown eyes weren't as beautiful as normal. "I got the map. I stole it from his desk. It has all these dots on it in the state. Not only dots, but arrows too."

"Why didn't you say nothing?" My inflection raised. I was mad at her for a minute.

She looked at me, a tear descended, and she spun and sprinted into the forest towards Millie.

"Wait," I called out to her and rushed to our hideaway. I caressed her face. "I'm sorry, Kat. I never even asked you and we ain't had a chance to look things over. Plus, you ain't ever been raised to think about nothing. You just been raised to follow and obey. Let's see that map."

She scurried back to where Millie lay sleeping and grabbed her small rucksack. She pulled out some papers, unfolded them and returned to me. We hurried over to where Josiah stood guard so that we all could look at it. The map was the same as my father's. Colored circles indicated the safe havens or conductors. The only difference was the arrows that highlighted an area near Nacogdoches and Lufkin, where we were heading. I grit my teeth in silence.

Kat spoke first. "Robert, maybe your uncle doesn't want me to think, but I'm human. I have me a brain." She turned her head toward her friend.

"Let's scoot on the edge of the forest and head south. We can stay hidden and make it here." Josiah pointed to a town on the southern fringe of the forest. We'd have to backtrack a few miles."

"Yeah, it might give us some time to let the posse get ahead of us."

"I thought your original plan was to outrun them."

"It was but your pa seems to be one step ahead of us. There's a reason he made me overseer. There was a reason he was selling Mill and Kat off, that is if he even planned on selling them. He might have suspected something and forced our hand. Now we need to change plans and keep them guessing.

"What are we gonna do?" Kat asked, her leadership qualities blooming with every challenge.

"Yeah, Robert. What are we gonna do?" Josiah prodded, poking a stick in my chest.

"This is the most dangerous part. We could out race them. Let's head west, maybe even bunk out here, in order to give them a couple of days ahead of us."

Kat's gaze questioned me.

Josiah stared at me, then her. "Robert, you wanted me to be the brains here. It's time we think this out." He paused to pace around the bayou, before kneeling.

Kat peeked at him with unabashed admiration before he continued, "Let's put the facts together. Right now, I see that my pa set us up for the escape. There is a reason he wanted us to attempt it."

I nodded and glanced at Kat who kept her focus on my cousin.

"Second, hell we need to retreat further into the bayou and stay hidden. The posse should be closing in on us if they chose this path. Third, Pa ain't joining the posse. He hit town and sent a telegraph around to the authorities. He wants his property back, dead or alive." He glanced down and Kat, and her expression showed no remorse. She wanted to run and could care less if she got caught. Being hung would be better than a return to her previous life.

Josiah continued, "I'm still not sure on which side Clete is on. He's the wild card in this. I'm sure he's behind a lot of this…"

I interrupted. "These markings on the map. Are those Uncle Zeke's or Clete's? Maybe these are routes he has taken, not where Zeke has a posse waiting."

They stared at me. Honestly the arrows were just scribbles and the penmanship could not be made out anyway.

"We can't take the chance. Robert, if you don't mind. I suggest we scoot down here to San Augustine." He pointed to the spot on the map. Can we get there tonight?"

"Let's go. I'll get the horses ready. You get your girl, and we'll take off."

"I need a little rest, since I've been on guard all this time. We'll still be good."

"Alright, head back to the camp with your girl. We'll stay out here and get organized for getaway."

Kat seemed afraid to speak. She hesitated and then blurted. "What if we split up? The two of us ride off now, and they can catch up. We meet at the dot here in two days. It should keep them guessing."

I glanced at Kat, then my cousin, who scratched his head, pondering on the idea. Josiah responded, "I like it. We'll stay here for another night. You guys can leave now, stay hidden or make a run to Jasper. We need some alone time anyway. Maybe you guys do too."

I looked at Kat. I ain't never done nothing with her except admire her baths and ripped clothes off her when called to whip her a couple of times. I hadn't done nothing to a woman, so I wasn't sure what to do. She met my eyes and smiled at my awkwardness. I felt confused as arousal took over and I felt the way I did when I see her bathe her body. I gathered up everything, then assisted her on my horse. She straddled it perfect, while I took a few more seconds to admire her before pulling myself on the horse. We rode off, skimming the range of the deep bayou. The sunlight flickered on and off, before we arrived at a village.

Among the few houses that rose into view, not one with a candle in the windows. This was not our destination, but only a place to hide out for a day. I missed my cousin. Finally, alone with Kat, I had no idea what to do.

We got to where we would exit the bayou and began to head to haven.

"Let's go further back here in the trees."

We pranced in the dark with no light at all, except the moonlight and starlight that could not penetrate the thickness of the swamp. Mild splashing under the hoofs announced a small stream. A few feet later it was dry. We made a camp. I undid my bedroll, and then heard Kat splashing in the stream. With no light to admire her beauty, I let my other senses explore her while we bathed together.

Chapter 8

Kat lay naked, wrapped in the blanket. I rubbed the dust from my eyes as morning broke. Our caressing felt awkward and unfulfilled but remained enjoyable. Staggering from the events of the previous night, I didn't fathom what I saw. A pistol aimed straight at me. My little cousin, Cletus Barnum, held it.

"Watcha doing here, Clete?"

"I'm bringing you back. There's a bounty for you and Pa says dead or alive." He clicked his revolver.

"You ain't gonna kill your only cousin. You just mad cause we took the girl you wanted to pop. Plus, your brother is back in woods."

"Josiah ain't in the woods. If I know him and he's my brother, he probably took a different route."

"I'm serious, Clete. We split up and wanted to play with Kat and Mill. Do you want me to call him? Josiah, Millie, are you ready to roll?"

No one answered.

"They must still be getting some shuteye, or she be pleasing him."

"I think you're lying to me."

The gun still pointed at my face. My cousin's hands shook. I knew he wasn't going to shoot me. I left my rifle back beside a sleeping Kat. I was hoping she'd rescue me this one time. I called for Josiah one more time.

"Josiah, your brother is here." I raised my voice, hoping to get Kat's attention.

She wandered in our direction holding my rifle. As far as I knew she'd never shot a gun before, but she didn't have to. If she could swing it hard, she could knock my little cousin flat, and we'd skedaddle.

"Josiah, come here."

"He ain't here damnit, Robert. I would have passed him and caught my double-crossing brother."

I saw Kat creeping up on, carrying my Remington and seized the moment that Clete turned away to search the forest to make a chopping motion with my hands which Kat noticed. She swung the barrel at Cletus and knocked him flat. Without wasting a second, I rushed forward to pick up his revolver.

"Take his horse, hop on and follow me."

Kat ran toward his horse, struggled on mounting it, but eventually got on as, she galloped off. I gathered our belongings and tossed everything into the bedroll, before scampering on the horse to ride beside Kat.

"How fast can you ride that thing?"

"Mastah Robert, I don't know how to ride. I'm a little scared."

"We just gonna ride a few miles down the path. We gotta stay in the forest unless you wanna make a run for the house with the lantern in daylight."

"I don't think I can ride that far."

"You'll climb on with me in a bit. I just want to get Clete's pony away from him. We gonna make him walk miles. We'll ride like this until we get to a clearing, then we could ditch his horse and you hop on this and hang on."

The land to the southwest of us was of a similar environment, one I was comfortable riding. Rivers we could swim across on horseback, swamps, and thick forests provided excellent hiding spots. However, the further south we went, the more the land started to clear out as swamps turned into grassland.

It took about an hour to arrive at a decent clearing. I pulled up the horse reins and instructed Kat to do the same on Clete's. After I helped her off, I fired Clete's gun in the air to get his horse to sprint off in the direction we would be heading. My cousin was now several miles back and might still be knocked out cold. We had a good four hours on him, but still judging by the sun, it was nowhere near high noon.

I glanced at Kat's beautiful soul with her dark skin. The only issue was I needed to cover that pretty face up because of the wanted posters up for the four of us. Her rucksack was tied with a bandana. I emptied her miniscule belongings and packed my bedroll even tighter, so that I could cover that lovely face with the bandana. I slashed my face with my knife, causing a scar that wasn't a perfect disguise, but would buy us time. I needed every precaution, and I didn't want to leave any stone unturned.

"Ready to ride. We'll be there by dark." I aided her on the horse and then climbed on board.

The animal was rested. I picked some berries and allowed the animal lap up water from the flowing stream nearby. These next few days would be the toughest. With only bandana and baggy clothes to hide her race, it was about to be all or nothing. Every calculated plan we had, we had to change. I kicked the horse in the side, and we galloped off.

The first town we hit was nothing more than a dust bowl with a few saloons and scattered people. We slowed down in order not to raise suspicion, and then stormed through, leaving trails of dust. At this pace, I figured we were about halfway to our destination. The sun had started its descent, placing the time at about two in the afternoon. The Neches River was to the west of us. We headed into the river basin for a break, and maybe a nap until dusk.

To ensure that the tracks couldn't be detected, we ride in the shallow stretch of the water by the riverbank, wondering away from civilization. I asked Kat to pull the bandana down so she could breathe easier and help me pick a place to bunk for a few hours.

"Robert, over there. Are those people?"

"Not sure but cover up just in case. I stalled the horse so I could give her time to cover that pretty face before we continued riding. Suspicion was the last thing I wanted. Her arms wrapped around my waist as we trotted along the edge. The closer we got, the more people we saw on the bank on the other side, scouting about.

I whispered, "I ain't talking to no one unless they speak to me. I'll be sure to tell a good ole lie about why we're riding." I hoped I didn't have to but was thinking about a good fib to tell these folks.

"Howdy, stranger?" a voice called out across the river.

Kat clung tighter to my belly. Her soft shrieks almost drowned the man's voice.

I tipped my hat to him. "Looking to do some trapping up the river a way. I need to get some pelts, make some new clothes. Any trading posts up the river?

"Yeah, there be a few of them not too far from here. If you want, I can ride up and show ya."

"Much obliged, but I'm an explorer. I like to find things myself. Pa says I can't find my asshole unless the shit was coming out." I tipped my hat again and we continued up the river until they were out of sight. We made a dash into the forest, while I hoped Kat was unseen.

I stopped to throw a couple beaver traps near a small dam the mammals created. We then found seclusion and privacy. I took the horse to the river to quench his thirst, while we scavenged for food. Rabbits were easy to come by, so shooting a couple wasn't a problem.

We laid back in the East Texas forest. Gauging by how far we'd come, I knew the town was only a few miles away. We'd be there in an easy hour. With it being dark out, the lantern in the window would be easier to spot. The folks who conducted these operations were braver souls than me. Yes, I fled with Kat, while my older cousin ran off with Millie. True we sought freedom, however the conductors who ran the railroad were just as guilty as the escapees. It's not known how many people would pass through a house at one time, whether there would be any protection. These houses could be raided at any time of the day or night, and the law was always welcome to raid a place.

I didn't have the exact location of the haven, but the map placed it in or around the village of Jasper. We were lucky, since darkness enveloped the East Texas town, but Kat still pressed her face covered by her bandana into my back.

"I need you to peek around and look for the lantern in the window. I'll watch out for catchers."

"I don't want to be seen," Kat replied, her voice frightened. "I'm getting scared being out in the open."

I bit my lip and swallowed hard. Death awaited both of us if we got caught. People were out and about, going from saloon to saloon. Right now, my hope was that they were too drunk to notice anything.

"I really need some help. Pull the bandana down from your eyes and sit back a for a minute and look around. I need you."

"Yes, Master." She craned her neck back and forth, checking out the houses as we pranced down the mud-packed street. The buildings thinned out as we approached more farmland, and we kept our slow trot.

"Up yonder!" she screamed. "On the other side of the road."

I glanced in at the direction she pointed and spotted the house with a sole lantern in the upstairs window. I nudged the horse to increase its speed a wee bit. It was nowhere near a gallop, we still trotted down the path but with more intensity.

"Good job, Kat." I peeked behind to ensure no one followed. I rode faster, this time a controlled gallop as we hit the property. The only light on was the upstairs lantern.

We dismounted and strolled up. I knocked on the door, using my body to shield Kat from anyone peeking around. A middle-aged gentleman answered. His graying hair, alongside his thick, long, bushy beard was on full display. He donned horned rim spectacle. He saw me first, then Kat and smiled as he whipped out a poster and showed it to us.

"You youngins look familiar," he said, taking another look at the poster. "I'm William James." He stretched out his hand for a handshake.

The poster said wanted dead or alive with just our picture on it and a $1000.00 reward. Josiah and Millie were not on display.

"Come on in. I'll get my boy to hide the horse in the barn."

I admired the artwork of the two of us.

"My other boy rides around and takes them off the saloon windows. The less exposure for you, the easier to flee."

"Why is this just us? My cousin and his gal also escaped."

He answered, "We got another one. It's just wanted alive, and a $500.00 reward."

"Looks like Zeke can't kill his own flesh and blood but will have no problem seeing his only nephew butchered up."

"I know who you guys are. You're the Barnum boy, your pa is the abolitionist preacher. Good man. This is like a hotel. Let me get you to your room and show you where your next stop is."

"How long can we hold up here? We're supposed to meet Josiah. We split up in route, but he should be here in a couple of days."

"Maybe a night or two. Posse has been around already. They found nothing but will always come back. I risk my life every day helping runaways get to Mexico. That's why we can't keep you for long, plus we never know when someone else is coming. We ain't got that much room. Maybe room for three parties, ten total people."

"Anyone else here?" Kat asked.

"Nope, you are the only ones right now. Let's head upstairs."

His son led us up the staircase into a small bedroom that I thought should have been bigger. The son, who was about my age, walked up to me with his hand on a heavy armoire.

"Can you help me slide this over yonder?" He pointed a few feet away.

I understood what he wanted and why. Pa told me a lot of these stations had hidden rooms, so I hurried over and helped shove the heavy piece of furniture several feet, exposing a trap door. I glanced at the exposed wall and saw nothing out of the ordinary, only the radiators that distribute the steam heat.

I looked around, scanning over the exposed area.

"Pull up on the radiator," the boy commanded.

I started pulling up on the steamer. I hoped this was a passage to safe keeping, since I didn't know how to open it. The boy looked at me, and then Kat.

Kat shrugged, huffed and came over. She reached down to the bottom of the radiator, and it lifted up, exposing a crawl space. Kat smiled at me, one in a teasing nature and wiped her hands. The boy went into the crawl space first. He crawled through the tunnel to a short set of stairs. After a climb of a few feet, he shoved on a door, and it opened. He led the way as we climbed inside a room that lay close to the ceiling. There was no standing room at all, only kneeling.

He explained, "That room we entered, well, we made the other half hidden. There are two more levels, all the same size with different entrances from the main room. Catchers have never found these rooms. They've been in the main room many times, pounded on walls, moved and chopped the furniture up, but still never discovered nothing."

I laid on my back as he crawled to light a lantern.

"I'll bring you a bite to eat and some water. One more thing, there's a back way out in case they find the tunnel. It's never been used except for runaways to use the toilet."

He slid a picture on the wall exposing a tunnel and had us crawl down some steps leading to a restroom downstairs, one that was completely hidden from the main house.

"I got a question," Kat said. "If someone comes in, can they hear us?"

I followed her question up, "Can we hear them marching around?"

"-The answer to both questions is yes. So, you do need to always stay quiet. No chit chat, no nothing. Remember you're fugitives in the eyes of the law. The only way they would know you're hiding out is by giving yourself away. So be quiet."

I liked this place. It was absolutely shut off from the main house, but still inside it. We climbed back in to hide out and wait for Josiah and Millie.

Chapter 9

The night was quiet as I held Kat in my arms, snuggled on top of me. We heard every squeak that echoed inside the house. At every small noise we heard, she clenched me tighter, until we eventually fell asleep.

The next morning, the son crawled through the entrance with some bacon and flapjacks for breakfast.

"Posse came around last night again. Pops didn't let them in the house, but they circled for about an hour. They got here right after you did. It ain't safe out there right now. You are welcome to stay if you like. We might shut the lantern off to protect you and us."

I took a piece of bacon and a bite of pancake. "What about Josiah? He should be here today or tomorrow. We will ride off once we meet him."

"Pops says it's too dangerous right now. The catchers are all over the land and around town. Rumors from the town folk say they thought runaways passed through, and heard a couple got caught."

"Kat shrieked. "Millie and Josiah?"

"Pops said it was a family. Got caught inside town this morning."

She bowed her head, and I heard her mumble. "Please God, not my family."

I held her so tight her body merged into mine.

"Pa was helping them get up the river. We weren't planning on sending them this way. Us four were going to Mexico, while the rest of your family was going to the Nations. Remember, we're not the only ones out there. We gonna be fine." I scratched her cheek and kissed it in front of the son.

The boy turned away, embarrassed. He must not have seen a white boy affectionately kiss a slave girl.

"You two can't be married?"

"That's why we're going to Mexico, same with my cousin and his gal, who is also a runaway. We need to wait, unless you think we can meet at the next stop."

"Ain't no others here yet. The woods have posse all over. I saw some riding around earlier, when I was out scouting. They plastered more posters of you two on trees. I'll check with Pa to see how long we'll keep you."

"Did you hear anything the catchers were saying?"

"Just bits and pieces, but I didn't want to get too close."

I inched closer to him on hands and knees since I couldn't stand up.

"They said something about seeing an older boy pointing a revolver at a young kid. Thought there was a runaway with him."

Kat turned her head away. I glanced at her then boy. "Josiah and Millie. They should be close, but they got Clete with them."

"I need to rassle them up. Got a couple partners." The kid took our plates and slipped out towards the main part of the house.

We sat in silence in exclusion in our hideaway from where we could hear the boy speaking to his father. Kat and I pressed our ears to a wall, hoping to hear more of the conversation."

The boy started. "Robert's cousin is nearby. I'm grabbing the Wills boys so we could go grab them."

"All three? I don't trust the youngest," the father spoke.

"I just want the two oldest. They ain't afraid to use a gun either. What Robert said is his youngest cousin is with him. We need to hijack him."

"Go, don't come back without the two. I'll work on getting these two ready to go. You can take the four horses, and the Conestoga wagon."

Silence fell across. I wished we could peek out a window, so we'd know what was going on. Kat and I snuggled under a blanket, feeling more secure.

Commotion interrupted the tranquility. We heard the screaming strangers' voices. "Where are they? You hiding the boy and the slave girl? We will search the property. Go search the barn and burn it down if we must."

"Marshall, I'm not hiding no one. Search the house."

Kat shrieked. I placed my hand on her mouth, squelching her gasp. She gazed at me in horror, then lowered her head in shame.

We heard them stomp through the home, slamming doors as they wandered throughout the house. The stomping got louder.

"What's this room?"

"Only a guest bedroom," the father answered.

The door slammed open.

"No one here," the man who seemed in charge shouted. "Jack, move that armoire."

"It's heavy, Marshall. Give me a hand."

"I promise you, there is nothing there," the father said.

We heard grunting and groaning as the armoire was shoved across the wooden floor, more than likely scratching the oak.

The Marshall continued, "there ain't nothing here. This room is mighty small, so there must be something behind it. Knock on the walls and see if it's been hollowed out."

We listened to tapping. And the Marshall rambling about something must be back there.

The other voice shouted out. "Sounds hollowed out like a hidden room. We can burn them out."

Kat buried her head into my arms.

"If you burn my house with no reason, you will be hung. I don't care if you're a US Marshall."

"What's behind this then?"

"I built a storm shelter with some crawl space; it can only be accessed from the outside. Let me show you."

We heard footsteps leaving but no one followed. I glanced at Kat, and she returned the peek. She had to be scared since I was. I wanted to make a dash, then again it would be a suicide run. I had to trust the homeowners.

A door shut and then there was nothing but silence. No voices echoed around. Soon we heard muffled voices coming from another direction. The father must have shown him around the place.

"Check the barn?" the Marshall said.

Then nothing. We relaxed and waited.

After an hour of silence, only isolated noises reached us. It sounded like one person. We sat up at attention as the noise of a body moved past the armoire, and there was the squeak of the radiator being moved and a person climbing. The hidden door opened, and the father crawled through the passageway.

"That was close," he said after exhaling. "They left but will return more than likely with torches. Robert, I'm gonna need some help. I need to move the wagon to the back barn, where your horse is hidden. I guarantee my boy will bring your cousin and his friend in within the next two days. Tomorrow night we'll move you to the back barn, so when they come storming in, we'll hitch you up and he'll take you to the next stop some twenty miles south of here.

I grabbed the wrinkled map from my bedroll, pointed to a yellowed town. "This the place?"

"Why does your Pa mark the colors? I'm green up here, this one is yellow."

"You can be trusted. This one can't. We'll need to be careful." I looked for another green dot further south. There was one west. "What about over across the Neches. Not sure if there is a ferry but I might find one close."

He hesitated and then stuttered. I began not to trust him, but I was a fugitive wanted by the law and bounty hunters. One wrong move would make me reward money for this man. A thousand- dollar bounty for me was impressive.

"I always send folks south. Now help me with the wagon."

He seemed too anxious for me. Kat handed me my saddlebag. My bullwhip, my rifle was there, along with my Bowie knife. Clete's revolver was also packed. I had a choice if needed.

I wiggled my finger, encouraging Kat to follow.

"I'm coming, Mastah Robert," she said, not wanting to be left alone.

"She needs to stay here," the father said. "Posse might still be out there."

"And I'm the wanted man. Dead or alive it says. It was a damn good drawing of me with my name clear as a sunny day. I'm not leaving her alone."

We got in an Old Texas stare down. I was fully armed but wasn't sure about him. One thing was clear though, that we wouldn't go anywhere if I failed to get the wagon ready. I wanted Kat with me in case we had to flee, since my trigger finger was itchy. "She's coming with me. We'll make sure no one sees her. I got protection." I displayed my rifle and knife.

"Cover her up!" he shouted, but his voice was weak and defeated.

We climbed down the crawl space. I grabbed a blanket, tossed it over her head, and pulled her close to me as went to the main barn, where the Conestoga sat. As far as I knew we were unseen, but I motioned Kat to crawl in the wagon. I helped her in so that she hid under bags of rice, beans and other produce.

"Now hitch these horses up!" Another command and I did as told.

After getting the horses connected to the tongue of the wagon, we bounced out in search of the back barn hidden in the East Texas forest. I took out all my arsenal. I waited for him to hop on or point me in the right direction, but he vanished. I had Kat and two horses, but I needed mine if I chose to ride off with her. I rode deeper into the forest and spotted a small barn. I stopped the wagon, latched the brake, grabbed my weapons, all four and prepared to use them.

Unlatching the door, I broke in with guns pointed in anticipation of an ambush but saw nothing. I went back to where my horse, Flash, waited. He stood in the stall tied up. I led him out to the front of the barn and dug Kat out of the back of the wagon.

"What are we gonna do?' she asked me, brushing herself off.

I stared into her brown eyes, scratched my head while mulling over her question. I no longer trusted this family, and the son taking us for a ride was out of the question. I wanted to run west, cross the river, but the father knew that's what we wanted to do. My gut told me he sent people south to get captured, and they'd share the reward.

"What do you think we should?" I asked her after I realized we might be set up for a trap.

"I think we should wait for Millie and Josiah for another day. I have a hunch we'll see them tonight."

"Come here." I beckoned at her to follow me. I led her to the back of the barn to see if there was an exit. I shoved on some back walls until a door popped open. "I got it. We'll shoot the kid and frame Clete for it, if he's with them, fire the guns to send the wagon rolling south."

"We don't have to kill anyone, just stuff them in the wagon, let the horses run free, then we go the way you want to go."

"I like your thinking. Now I think we need to keep you hidden in the back of the barn. I'll tell them you're hiding already. Josiah and me will knock out Clete and the kid who helped us. We'll send the wagon south and we'll head west. The father already knows the boy will be driving the wagon, so he ain't gonna suspect a thing. No shooting unless needed."

We waited in the barn as nightfall enveloped the building. We sat in the front. Flash was near the rear exit, and my saddle roll already packed on his saddle. My weapons in hand, we waited. Kat sat beside me, holding her knees with her hand. I wrapped an arm around her, holding her close. I could barely see her face, but she never looked more beautiful to me than she did now. I held her face, studied its smooth curves and then kissed her pouty lips, aware I couldn't take things further.

As the kissing continued, hands wandered over each other's bodies as soft moans escaped from the two of us.

"Robert," she whispered. "Go ahead and touch me. I want you too."

I loved this little lady. My hands touched every crevice, until something in the air told me to wait.

Commotion echoed through the forest, quickly followed by gunshots. I hurried her to the back of the barn.

Hoofs pounded. I crept outside and shouted, "Josiah! Is that you."

My voice echoed through the trees.

Kat whispered, "Wait until we hear the song. Millie should be singing to me."

Off in the distance a faint tune crooned. I couldn't make out anything, however Kat recognized the voice and the words.

"Well, I'm sometimes up, and I'm sometimes down

Comin' for to carry me home

But but I know my soul is heavenly bound

Comin' for to carry me home"

"It's them. She is singing *Sweet Low, Sweet Chario't.* That's our code to each other." She smiled as she spoke.

A minute later we heard them ride up with, "Robert, I made it."

He stopped the horse, throwing Clete off in the same motion. Millie got off too. She snuck into the barn after I told her Kat hid in the back.

"Where's the boy?"

"Dead. Clete shot him and his two partners. A third boy came after us, but we made plenty of room."

My younger cousin made his way to us. You convinced I'm on your side now?"

I looked at Josiah with authority. He knew who was in charge. "I believe ya."

I swung the rifle barrel at his head, knocking him on the ground. He came to minutes later.

"We're stealing this wagon. The girls are hidden. Climb in, I'm driving the rickety thing."

Josiah didn't question me. Clete climbed under gunnysacks of produce where he stayed hidden. I smacked the belly of the horse with the same part of the rifle I used to beat my younger cousin with, then fired it in the air. The wagon vacated the property. We snuck through the barn and headed west on horseback.

Chapter 10

Josiah couldn't kill his brother, and neither could I, even though I wanted to. I had a reward for me, dead or alive, and Josiah was to be taken alive. I didn't want a murder rap to go with slave stealing. Killing wasn't in my nature. I would if I had to, and slave stealing shouldn't be against the law. Our girls were not property in the eyes of The Lord. They were human beings, and we had plans to marry them. I knew God was on our side.

"The father's gonna be looking for his boy soon. We need to get riding," Josiah said.

"We're gonna head west." I unrolled my map. "The place is Woodville, about thirty miles west with the lantern." I glanced at the sun that had dropped halfway.

"Must be close to three. Damn right, Josiah, we need to skedaddle."

We gathered up our ladies and headed out on horseback again. The wagon would have been nice, but any posse would search for the wagon if that man from Jasper was a traitor.

We hightailed out of the barn through the back way. With both gals clinging to our bellies, we meandered through the forest. According to the map we had, there was a stream about half-way. The sketch showed no clearing. It was all bayou and forest as we ambled across small streams and zigzagged through the trees. The larger creek was coming. I could hear the water flowing as I lifted the reins to halt the steed.

Josiah came up behind me. Kat continued clutching onto me and Millie clung to her man. Both horses stuck their snouts in the stream, needing no encouragement to start lapping up the water.

"We gonna bunk here for the evening, or do you think it's best to cross?" Josiah asked.

The girls walked around to stretch their arms and legs. We admired admiring their shape, both unaware of our gaze as they stole deep relaxing breaths.

"No, we gotta cross in case a posse comes. It shouldn't be too deep, but if the posse comes from the east, we can get moving faster. Remember, they be aiming to shoot three of us."

Josiah's usual jovial smile turned into a sneer. "Tired and trigger-happy posse don't care who they shoot. Me and you look the same from fifty to a hundred yards. Let's rest a bit, find the toughest and easiest place to cross this creek, and sneak into the forest near the strongest and deepest current. Then we can separate a bit, keep guard and have some privacy with the girls."

Josiah glanced over his shoulder, checking for anyone. He only saw the three of us and planted a kiss on Millie's lips.

I followed suit and took notice of Kat's beautiful eyes and lips and kissed her. "We're gonna do this, darling." I whispered in her ear. "We're gonna do it." She pressed her body into mine. "Pops told me the first challenge will be the toughest."

She stepped back and closed in again. "Why is that Robert?"

"Well now, we know what to look forward to. We can't trust a soul, only each other, and you got us out of several jams already."

"Do you trust Josiah?"

I glanced over at him, and Mill undressed and swimming in the river. "I do because I have to. He's smart, but sometimes too trusting. I don't think he should play around now. We're still not safe and won't be until we cross the border."

"Relax, Master Robert," she said. "Let's join them in the river. It's my job to care for you too. That's what a wife is supposed to do."

We strode over towards Josiah and Millie and noticed their clothes laying on a rock next to the river, however we didn't spot them. We tore off our apparel, dropped them in the flowing stream, washed out some of the grub and splashed water on each other, all the while giggling and laughing. The water seemed shallow enough to cross at this location. Kat and I tossed our clothes on a rock to dry, then swam off to wash each other's body in the flowing water. We touched where, legally and by the laws of God, we weren't supposed to. Since Kat didn't care, I didn't either, so our playfulness picked up. I relaxed, feeling like an authentic man, not the inexperienced heathen like It was the first time we attempted to make love, or I should say the first time for the creepy little kid who spied on her as she got naked in a washbasin on my uncle's plantation.

Locked in each other's arms on the other side of the river, naked without a worry in sight, I heard a noise. It sounded like twigs and sticks cracking, with the ruffling of leaves in the forest.

"Robert!" Josiah called. "Get the horses! We ain't alone here. Catchers are out there, due west. Not sure if they spotted me, but they probably heard me now. Let's get going."

Kat and I swam across the river. It was a spot where the horses could wade across. Maybe four feet at the deepest. We tossed all our gears on the back in the saddlebags and tossed them at the back of the saddle.

"Can you ride?" I asked as I hoisted Kat onto Josiah's steed.

"Of course, Mastah Robert."

"Follow me, Darling." I said, looking over my shoulder as the horses pranced into the river.

We met Josiah on the other side and tossed them their clothes. Dressed in record time, Josiah and Millie mounted.

"Which way?" I asked.

"The ones we heard, and saw were due west of us. Go south and we can circle around them."

I led again as horse and riders galloped on the west end of the river. I searched for a trail to head towards shelter. Josiah kept pace. I found a path running parallel to the river, Josiah remained on my trail.

"There they are. Fire." The voices came from the clearing.

Bullets ricocheted off Pecan trees. Kat shrieked, then her hand gripping my chest attempted to crack my ribs. I wanted her safe. I wanted the foursome safe as I wandered away from the stream.

I pushed the steed harder, cutting in and out of the forest and pushing further south than what I wanted. Another clearing arrived. We galloped through it as a small bayou appeared. Pecan trees turned into Cypress. The bayou was the perfect place to hide. About fifty yards in, large reptiles crawled along the shore and cruised the river. I halted the horse and crew.

"It's safer in this bayou than out there. I'm thinking we can stay in here. The posse won't come looking for us. I'll kill a gator for food, and clothes and make a bow, with some arrows and nail a deer. We'll have to stay in this thicket for a week and hope this posse moves away or gives up. Slaves are always escaping. These catchers want easier work."

"Clete's a bayou rat too, don't forget." Josiah interrupted my speech, so I needed a rebuttal.

"We can manipulate him. He has split loyalties to us and your father. We can use him to help, then send him off again and abandon him here if we run into him again. Remember, he's just a kid and wanted to be a part of this. He will jump at any chance."

"He should be on the other side of this bayou somewhere," Josiah spoke as we searched for place to bunk, which wasn't alligator infested.

"I don't trust that little brother of yours." I peered down the stream. "Is this the Neches again?"

"Yeah," Josiah replied.

"I got a plan; though we'll need the girls' help as well. It's gonna be hard work but look for some downed logs. We'll need about fifteen. We can raft down the river as far as we can. I was thinking about canoes, but I ain't abandoning the horses."

"I was thinking that, too. You and me can build the raft. I think Mil and Kat can dig out a canoe. Me and Mil will paddle behind you guys."

"Should be plenty of downed logs since a storm passed through."

"We spotted enough logs from the down trees as we rode through."

We searched and found a grove of birch, where there were a few trees downed by storms a few days ago. Done measuring the logs, we chopped them up. The plan was to make a navigable raft and one canoe. After chopping, we dragged the wood towards the river where I tied them up with a rope so the logs wouldn't separate.

Millie took over the chopping with Josiah's hatchet "I've done this before for Mastah Zeke." She smiled, informing us of her skills. "I'm gonna get this dugout in no time and get a pointy end on it, too. She took to cleaning the wood out and tossing the kindling to set up a campfire.

We all snagged knives and sticks, then proceeded to shave larger branches into a bow, and the sticks into arrows. Arrowheads and other stones got dug up for the tips, plus we used longer branches as spears. Kat wandered about, hoping to shoot up or stab some food. We needed little, plus gators infested the area. Pops and I would usually bag a couple a year and used everything for boots and belts. We were on the run and wouldn't have room on the raft for a big gator. Josiah and I chopped away on some logs, making them almost even and dragging them next to the river.

"Robert," Kat shrieked.

I ran over toward the direction of the scream. I didn't think it was a posse out searching or even my cousin. I suspected a critter of some sort, and if it was small, she wouldn't be screaming.

I rushed towards Kat, rifle in hand. A nice healthy six-foot gator was about sixty feet from here. A busted arrow lay beside it, and the gator looked mad. Kat retreated from it, unable to get further. I assessed the situation fast and was behind the beast as it moved in on her. I rushed towards her, but with caution. Shooting a gator needed precision. Josiah and Millie rushed towards me screaming. I got directly behind it, aimed behind the brain and pulled the trigger. I reloaded. The first shot ricocheted off the beast's thick skull. It wasn't dead, but angrier. I aimed again, squeezed the trigger, and reloaded. For good measure, I fired again, unsure which of the shots did it but it lay dead.

I approached carefully, pistol loaded and knife out. Josiah and Millie returned to work on the watercraft. I jabbed my knife in the soft spot, twisted it around, making sure the beast was dead. The passion I had for killing the beast was unmatched. My lips jutted out as I grimaced with every twist and turn. I was afraid I enjoyed killing this beast too much. It was either that or watching it devour Kat. I relaxed on the ground once I knew it was safe. She ran to me and kissed me.

"You saved my life, Mastah Robert. I love you."

"That's what I've been doing this last week. I'm saving your life to start one with you and I'm positive you will save mine on this journey."

We walked towards Josiah and Millie, who were hard at work digging out the canoe and tying up the logs, while our horses rested.

"I bet you know how to skin this thing. If you don't want to, take over for Mil. I'll clean it up. We'll need you to help with the raft or canoe."

"Yes, Robert." She moved over, leaving me to cut the skin off, salvage the meat from the tail and what I could from the skin. I shot it up pretty good. One miss and three shots through the brain did it.

After an all-nighter of finishing and testing the boats, plus cooking, cleaning, and eating gator tail, I fetched the horses and led them to the raft. Josiah, Millie, and I pushed the raft into the river, and I hopped on, joining Kat and both horses.

My cousin and his gal crawled into the canoe, tying it to the raft so we could tow them down the Neches. Satisfied that all was onboard, I grabbed the map out of my saddlebag and read it by torchlight as we drifted south through a thick bayou. I was on the lookout for any houses with lanterns near the end of the bayou.

Kat and I took turns sleeping and steering the raft. I gave her a crash course on using a carved log to guide the raft down the river and then I stretched out on the logs with my hat down over my eyes. Face partially hidden; I pondered on the day's events. Kat was a quick learner. She yanked the carved log from my grip and guided our makeshift raft down the river with a perfection that left me marvelling at her leadership traits.

I was determined to make Mexico. The raft would make the trip easier, since the horses and the four of us could rest and we'd be a lot closer to Mexico when we got off. We had food and some hides that Josiah could try to sell when we found a trading post.

I laid on the back of the raft, hat over my eyes.

"Robert, that gator really scared Jesus out of me. I have seen firsthand Josiah's daddy feed some orphans to them for bait and had a mama killed cause her husband ran away but got caught. Mastah Zeke made sure both mama and daddy got killed, and I saw the watchman come and gather up their four babies and fed them. I knew then I was leaving and I'm glad you took a liking to me and glad you ain't that way. Thank you, Robert." She knelt beside me and kissed my forehead. The raft drifted down the river and I drifted off for a deserved rest.

Chapter 11

The raft plunked into a dock. Kat did a good job guiding the raft down the river, but she stirred the boat all night and had fallen asleep. The canoe crashed into the dock, startling an elderly negro man out fishing.

"You runaways?" The older black man asked as we tried to gather our surroundings. He looked at a flyer, scanned the poster with aged eyes, and then checked it over. "Some young boy gave me this raggedy piece of paper earlier this morning. Mighty big reward for you kids."

From the canoe Josiah asked. "What did this boy look like?"

The old man considered the question. "Looked a lot like you, but younger." He peered at Josiah, acknowledging a resemblance.

"How long ago was this?" I asked, trying to distract him from his scrutiny of Josiah.

He glanced at the sky. "Judging by the sun, I'm gonna say a couple of hours ago. He rode off heading in that direction." He pointed west, which is where we aimed ongoing.

"Cletus." I glanced at Josiah. "He's still following us." I returned my gaze to the man, not leaving the raft. "You free, or a slave?"

"I am a slave, young man."

"You know any safe spaces for runaways here?" I felt like I could trust him.

"That white boy asked the same question. I don't trust the white boy, so I lied to him. Told him there was one west of town. The only white man I trust is Master."

I glanced around and so far, the older slave, his age was about sixty, was still the sole person about. Other townspeople trickled by in their buggies occasionally. We lay down when we noticed town folks trotting through.

"Do you trust us?" Josiah asked testily.

"Don't know you kids yet," came the defensive tone. "I shouldn't trust ya, since you're wanted and thieves..."

Kat cut in. "They aren't thieves. We are running away to get married and start a life in Mexico."

Millie nodded in agreement with her friend.

"Is that so? Maybe I trust you more. Do you trust me?" He asked but carried on without waiting for an answer. "I know a place to hide out."

Our ears perked up. Josiah and Millie jumped into the river from their little canoe and climbed up on the raft. "Where is this place?" Millie asked.

"Master's place," he said.

"He owns you; how do you trust him not to turn us in? We are wanted and bounty hunters and Texas Rangers be looking for us," I said.

"I know my master. He don't like this slavery thing any more than you or I do. He helps get folks to the next safe place."

"Can we talk about this as a group? We got four lives which aren't ready to die. We've made it from North Central Louisiana with still a long way to go. Posse's been following us and I'm sure there is more."

"I promise you, young men. I ain't got no reason to lie to you. Money means nothing to me. Master got money, he don't need it."

"I think we should take a chance. Clete's in the area, and I trust this man more than your brother."

"Hell with this man. He's a crazy old coot." Josiah took charge.

Kat and Millie looked at each other, both wanting to say something, but the cat got their tongue.

I heard Kat stutter.

"Say something," I told her.

She looked at all of us including the old man. "This man ain't lying. My gut says so. Let's follow him."

"Thank you, Kat. I was afraid to say something, but I got a feeling too," Millie said.

Josiah shrugged. It wasn't his decision but mine.

"Where is this place?" I asked the man.

"It ain't too far away. I can go get the buggy so you all can hide. I be leaving right now. Set the raft and canoe free and stay by the dock and I be back in minutes."

The old man gathered up his few possessions, stuffed them in a sock and twisted the end of his footwear into a knot. He twirled it around in a circle as he walked away.

"You trust him?" I asked Josiah.

"I'm still not sure. Millie and Kat got a good read. It must be that sixth sense or comradery from being slaves."

"Same thing I was thinking. We gotta trust their instinct in such situations. You gonna cut the rafts loose?"

"Not until we see that buggy, he says he's got."

"We don't trust him then. Ain't this like Jesus as our fathers preach? We need a shot of faith. Ain't no gators, and I see lots of Negroes strolling. They might be freed or slaves with passes. Kat, can you take the horses to the end of the dock, so you and Mil can keep an eye on them? Josiah and I still need to hide."

She came to the raft, grabbed our saddle bags, and led the horses off the rickety dock.

With the canoe and raft cleared off, I cut the rope which held the two boats and shoved the smaller canoe into the current where, if lucky, it would make the gulf. Otherwise, it would crash on the shore in southeast Texas, become a clue for a posse, and hounds will search for us nowhere near our current location. Josiah and I both swam under the raft, pulling the buoyant logs into the current before setting it free as it chased the canoe down the Neches.

We swam back to the dock, mostly underwater, and reached the dock. Kat and Millie sat on the end with the horses tied up and the saddle bags attached.

"He's showing up," Millie told Kat. "I got a feeling about this man. I wonder if we are from the same tribe back in West Africa. I felt something like we kinfolk somehow."

"He might be. I hope he tells us his story. My daddy never told us his story; except that he was born here."

"I know my daddy came on a ship," Millie said. "Daddy said pirates got it and they arrived in Texas somewhere. Daddy was just a boy then. Grandaddy didn't survive the ship. Pappy told me pirates got him, but that he wanted them scavengers to capture the ship."

We listened to them talk as we floated in the river. Both girls began to cry.

"We ain't ever going to see them again, are we?" Kat asked her friend.

"I don't think so, unless some miracles happen, but I want to be with Josiah forever and he promised to marry me. We will live in Mexico."

"Robert and I gonna be married too and start a family. I want lots of babies with him. Maybe our babies will be free."

Josiah and I swam up to the girls and dragged them into the river so that we all splashed the Neches on each other.

The man rode up on the buggy pulled by a single horse when there was room for two more. The girls ran up to join him, while my cousin and I followed at a more cautious pace.

"Boys, you ride under them blankets. I'm gonna get the girls to hitch up the horses. Mighty fine stallions you got here. They come in handy when running from the white man."

We scooted towards the back. Our guts didn't trust the man, but both our fathers were men of cloth who preached the word. Neither Josiah nor I were overly religious, but we understood the concepts. Faith, it is true we trusted our gut too many times, but we also needed faith and so far, Kat and Millie showed faith in this man.

Buried under a stack of blankets, with the girls riding up front, we overheard the boisterous speaking of the tall man talking to our ladies. "How you come here? I feel like I know you from somewhere." He spoke with the dialect of the locals we fled from.

I heard Kat stutter, afraid to talk to him or ashamed she was clueless about her heritage. To cover up her friend's awkwardness, Millie spoke up, "The boat pappy came over on got hijacked when he was a boy. Pirates stole the ship."

"You don't say. Same thing happened to me. We went to another island and landed on an island in Texas."

"Daddy said the same thing. You don't suppose you were on the same ship?"

"I bet we were. Where did your daddy come from?"

"West Africa; I'm sure Poppy says we were Igbo. I heard stories about this other tribe, the Aros. The Aros sold us to the white man."

"We be the same. Might be kin somehow. My poppy was an Igbo chief and Aros stole him and sold him way back when."

There was silence except for the clip clop of the horses' hooves. Kat, having regained her voice, spoke up. "How much further?"

"It's around the bend."

The buggy stopped; we heard voices.

"Sock, you got a pass, sir?" A voice we didn't recognize asked.

"I got me a pass, and a pass for these girls, too. Master asked us to get some fish, but we didn't catch nothing. He wants me to teach these girls how to fish. That's why they are with me."

I didn't like his story, since it sounded like he was making it up as he went.

"Go on, tell Master Dickerson hello."

"Will do," came the jovial voice of the older slave.

"See girls, be courteous and nice. My Master is good, but me and him heard stories. I got more freedom than most here in Beaumont. I don't mind living with him since he protects me. He wants to set me free, but then I be a target, and so would he. Life of a freed man ain't much better than a slave."

Kat asked, "So you're a free man, pretending?"

The man said nothing. I pictured him grinning at Kat and Millie as the buggy continued bouncing down the road. We felt it take a couple of quick turns, as it never increased in speed as we remained buried. Another turn and the wagon stopped.

"You wait right here while I go check with the boys in the back, and then with Mastah Dickerson."

He tapped on the wagon to the rhythm of old spirituals Uncle Zeke's possessions sung at night, not in English but of an African dialect. We lifted our protection over our bodies, and the tall slave busted out in laughter.

"Surprise, boys. We made it to Master Dickerson's home. Stay here while I drive this into the shed. I need to let Mastah know you are here."

He removed the blankets so that we could peek around. Millie led the horses into a barn adjacent to a small house. She stopped the carriage inside, and she and Kat climbed on the bales of hay at the back of the small barn. Josiah and I joined them.

Both ladies leaned back, relaxed. Josiah grabbed Mill's hand. He was ready for more of their private time.

She resisted. "No, not now. Not in this man's, who we haven't met, barn."

My cousin pressed. "It's been days now. You didn't want to in the skiff, cause you were afraid we'd tip it. Now you're afraid of...?" He didn't finish.

"We just got here. This man is gonna help us. He might not help us if you got your thing in me. Let's wait until after we talk to him or the old man."

"What if this is a trap? I won't get any loving in before you three get yourself killed, and I'm hauled back to the stockade and branded a thief. Remember that traitor Clete is around. I want you now." Josiah's voice rose, the more Millie refused him.

I always respected my older cousin, but this time he was in the wrong.

He grabbed her arm and attempted to pull her up so they could hide for a few minutes to do their thing, but Millie planted her feet firmly.

103

"C'mon Mill!" He screamed. "I need you."

He tried to pull her along.

"Stop, leave me alone. I don't want touched right now."

Josiah tripped her to the ground and climbed on her. She shrieked for help, so I ran and threw my cousin off her.

"Stop it. We don't know when that man is coming back. Hell, she might be related to him from what we overheard. Be patient. If he or the Master sees you banging her, he might toss us out. Remember, under the raft, we decided to have faith in this man. He might be Jesus, he might be the devil, either way he is part of our plan."

"Wait a minute, hotshot. We're both in charge. And I want my woman now."

"Well, she said no."

Kat and Millie curled up in the corner.

"You ain't any better than your Pa making the girls submit. Millie, you gonna let him once we all get comfortable, okay? I bet this is where we will hide out, so Kat and I can find a place of our own."

Kat smiled at me.

"Mastah Robert, I love you being the man." She still held her friend even as Millie and my cousin argued. The argument continued until Josiah weakened on seeing his fiancé burst into tears. He rolled over to a far edge of the loft and sat with his head between his knees.

Bored with his thoughts, he strolled towards the three of us.

"Mill," he got on a knee, "I'm sorry. I was so hyped up and needed to feel you. It helps me relax and you know that, but I didn't want to force you. We're gonna make it to Mexico and get married, and even then, I can't force myself on you."

She patted the straw beside her. "Can you hold me, Josiah? I need to feel safe in your arms. That's another way to show your love. Hold me and make me feel safe."

He moved down next to her and wrapped his arms around her, while pulling her body close. He kissed her forehead, then her cheek, and finally the lips. She rested her head on his lap. I took mental notes and held Kat the same way while we waited.

Chapter 12

Sock returned with an elderly white man, who was shorter than the slave, but Sock was a tall man, towering over six feet. The man was dressed nice; not aristocratically, but his wardrobe didn't appear like he dressed to work the fields either. He glared at me. "You the fugitives I heard about; I take it? Mighty big reward out for ya."

All four of us looked at each other, then his slave, and back at Mr. Dickerson. We waited for one another to speak. Josiah cleared his throat, but I cut him off.

"We be them," I said. "Is this a safe place to bunk out for a day or two?"

"It is now. Ol' Sock here told me about you. Says he was on the same ship as the one girl's kin. I used to think what we were doing wasn't that bad, but I heard my man's story and realized how wrong it was. We got an arrangement. He remains my worker, I give him a place to stay, three meals a day, which he cooks and his own quarters. In turn, he does chores, however I give him several passes so he can go fishing or do his own chores. If I give him his freedom, he's gonna be free, but can't live with me."

"We're going to go to Mexico." Josiah confessed. "We got plans to marry these ladies."

"You still got a long way to go, but once you get past Houston, it will get easier. Lots of Mexicans live there and they don't like white folk. They will help you."

"What about getting help to Houston?" I asked. "Any safe places to bunk out?"

"I got a map here. My place ain't even on it."

We glanced at the map, and I noticed a place just inside The Chambers County line.

"Josiah, grab the maps my pa gave us. I want to compare the two."

He went back and grabbed my saddlebag and pulled it out. We studied them for any differences.

"Same map. Clete has a copy, and he was here."

The man looked at me, then at Josiah. "Who is Clete?"

"My little brother." Josiah answered. "He's been trying to double-cross us since before we started. He knows about this place." Josiah pointed to the dot on the map about thirty miles to the southwest."

"Some young boy was here on horseback asking about a couple of kids and a couple of slave girls. He said the girls were his pa's property, and he wants them back. He gave me this reward poster." The man scanned the poster and then studied Josiah and me. "Damn good sketch of you two." He showed us the artwork. "Sock hadn't told me about you yet."

"How long ago did he leave?" I asked.

"He left here right before Sock came rolling in. Must be an hour now."

I looked at the rest of my group. "I can catch him and make sure he doesn't track us down."

"You ain't killing my brother." Josiah approached me with clenched fists.

"I ain't gonna kill him. I'm smarter than him. If you're smarter than someone, you don't need to do no killing. I'll need another lasso; I'll tie him to a tree, or I'd take him to the Marshall's office and tell him he's wanted and after that I'd shack up in that place and meet you there."

"No, Robert. I need you with me." Kat pleaded.

"He's always one step ahead or one step behind us." While my gaze begged Kat for approval, I glared at Josiah, feeling a hint of mistrust toward my partner. "I can make up an hour easy. He ain't that quick on a horse." I glanced around the barn, illuminated only with a lantern. "What should I do to him when I catch him? I'm thinking about taking him to the law and have him arrested for stealing Zeke's property. That should clear us for a few days, too. At least get us into Houston."

"It's a big city. There's about 4,000 people there and it would be easy to blend in. One thing I tell others is to not look scared in the big cities. Don't run scared. I know of places to hide out or blend in. Young man, I think it's a good idea. Sock, why don't you make some lunch for these kids, and bring this man another rope," Mr. Dickerson said.

The old black man took off towards the house. I smeared some mud on my face and unhitched the pony from the buggy. It's been a few days since I pushed him hard, and I knew he wanted to sprint. Sock returned with a quick lunch for us. I hadn't eaten that good since we left, so we all sat in the barn and ate a slab of pork ribs, applesauce, beans and vegetables. It was the best food I ever ate. I didn't want to leave the others, however; I felt they were in excellent hands. After scarfing the meal and visiting the outhouse, I returned to kiss Kat goodbye. I took off after glancing at the map. I knew my way around South Texas. I always did.

The man said don't ride like you're terrified, ride like you belong there. I wasn't fearful as we trotted through town. Once the buildings vanished, I did too, as I picked up the pace. The sun had moved to the western sky. I kicked the horse, and it went faster, thankful to me as it was ready to run.

Gone were the thick bayous with cypress trees. We abandoned them before the raft crashed into the dock on The Neches. I never had time to check the land out. I was in a new territory for myself, but one I enjoyed. The land was more prairie and marshes, and I could make plenty of time.

After three hours of hard riding straight on a cart path, I was sure I had made up time. I found a stream, fed the horse, and led him to the creek to lap up some water. Once he was done and I finished a snack, we high tailed out and continued the journey, continuing the southwest sprint with increased vigor.

Another hour passed with no sight of him. I prayed there was a nice hill we could climb, so I'd get a good look over the valley. The land was flat, with a slight uphill slope, not enough to notice, but as we rode up, I saw some rolling hills and galloped up one and then the next. At the crest of the second and biggest hill, I yanked the reins, halting my beast.

I looked over the valley with the field glasses resting on my nose. Scanning the valley, I saw a rider. It had to be my cousin. He wasn't riding fast; I figured I could catch him in another hour. I checked both sides of where he rode and found paths where I could pass him and wait. This was going to be too easy. I was slightly worried but was on my way.

My horse and I galloped down the hill and scaled the next one before I maneuvered the horse off the main trail, zigzagging through the forest. I kept this up for an hour and then moved back on the main path. Not sure if I had passed him, I searched the path for hoof prints but saw none. I must have passed him and ventured into the trees. It shouldn't take long.

Standing a couple of trees in the thicket, I didn't wait for long. Through the field glasses, I saw a boy riding up. Cletus

Barnum would no longer be a fly on shit for us. I still wasn't sure what to do with him. A ride to the Rangers of Marshal's office put me at a greater risk. I was the wanted kid.

As he got closer, I could see his head shake back and forth. I untied my horse and rode to the center of the path. The sun now setting behind me. I had an edge. The horse and I were stationary, and the lasso in hand with the rifle ready if needed. Despite that I was handy with ropes, whips, knifes and a rifle, Clete could shoot decent, quicker and more accurately than me.

He didn't stop as I rode to him.

"Cletus Barnum!" I hollered. "I found this picture of you. A wanted poster for stealing some slaves back in Louisiana. You're a fugitive, and there's a bounty for you. I'm taking you in.

"Robert Barnum, you're the wanted one," he said, acknowledging me. "I ain't gonna kill my kin." He reached for his revolver.

Mine sat loaded in the holster. I removed the pistol from its holster and fired, knocking the pistol from his hand. I tossed the lasso out, roped the boy in one movement and yanked the brat off his horse. He tumbled into the vegetated path. I dismounted and strode towards him as he laid wrapped up.

"Why are you doing this? I'm on your side. I've been helping." The boy pleaded still laying on his back.

"You've been trying to set us up this entire time. You want reward money."

"I've been on your side. I got the overseer fired so you could get the job, making it easier to escape."

"Save your breath." I continued to tie him up. With the rope tightly wrapped around his arms and legs, flipped his body on the horse. His legs and arms flailed all over. I wrestled him and tied the horses together so his beast would follow mine. I picked up his weapon, then rode off down the road, wondering who and where the law was around here.

I rode in the open, not worrying about being caught. My kid cousin and I had similar features. He wasn't involved in the stealing; however, he would pay the consequence if caught. I rode into the sunset; the giant fire due west painted a panoramic view in the western sky. If I was on track, there should be a house with a lantern or candle in the window. I needed more darkness as we neared the village.

A few houses appeared as I rode into the valley. Five, from what I could see. I wasn't sure which one was the safe spot. My horse and I led Clete's horse into the village and paraded around the homesteads. On seeing the lantern, I glanced at my tied-up cousin, now frantic about where to dump him.

The gas lantern was at the window when I crept over to the house. I carried my wanted poster with me as Clete plopped off my horse onto the moist soil, and I followed the man's eyes as they observed my cousin tumble.

"Who are you?" he asked, looking me all over.

I showed him the wanted poster I swiped from Cletus. "They're in Beaumont. I told them to get here tomorrow."

"Who's that kid?" He nodded towards Clete.

"My kid cousin. He wanted to be part of this, but I can't trust him, never could. I need to dump him off with the law, tell them he's a wanted man."

"Law is back a way. First place you dropped by, go dump him and be back."

"Where do I dump him?"

"Head down south, land turns into a swamp, and be right back."

We galloped towards the gulf. The further south we traveled, the more the vegetation and soil changed. We soon hit swamps similar to the vegetation we left in Louisiana. I had no plans of killing Clete. I made sure he had his saddle bag packed and loaded on his horse. He might be a few hundred yards away, lost in the swamp from the steed, but that wasn't my problem.

I rode further into the swamp and tied his horse up and loaded the bag on the saddle, remounted and turned around. Riding back to where the trees thinned out, and soil was dryer, I tossed him off and loosened the knots. I tore off his bandana so he could see me.

I pointed my colt at him. "Head back to your daddy's and quit following us. You ain't coming with us." I turned my aim to a slithering snake winding through the swamp and shot it dead. The snake flopped in the air before tumbling into the mud. "I don't miss." I kissed the tip of the pistol and blew the smoke away. Then I mounted the beast and rode away to meet the man at his house. I scarfed, got cleaned up and waited for Josiah, Kat and Millie. Cletus too. I never trusted him.

"How long can we stay here?"

The man, a quaker preacher, knew my pa and had nothing but good words for him.

"My job is to get you to the next place. You got to go to Houston. It's a hard day's ride. It's best in two. Plenty of freedmen there too, so blending in is possible. The main trail runs through. Law is heavy and they will look for you. Ezekiel Barnum is well known and well hated or well liked, depending on your point of view."

"It's best we take a cart then to keep the girls covered and make it to Houston in two days."

He interrupted. "Let's look over the map."

We strolled into his office, which had a roll-top desk. There he pulled out the hand-drawn map scrolled onto brown paper with sketches of the area.

"Ain't nothing between here and Houston. Just these two inlets here." I pointed to Trinity and Galveston Bay. "Might be safer, but an extra day to sneak around the water. More places to blend in."

He studied me like we were playing cards. "You're a freethinker, and that's good. A trip like this requires both outstanding planning and quick thinking, since you don't know what's coming next."

I prepared for the set-up and turned my head in search of the quickest exit. Kat was the only one I could trust, since sometimes I doubted Josiah and Mil. At this point, I wondered if I would be the downfall of the journey. So far as it goes, Kat had bailed me out a few times already, and I'm glad she'd be my wife.

Chapter 13

Two days passed and I ain't heard a word from my party. Hiding out wasn't an option now. Riding back to Beaumont would be my best option, but a younger cousin I've tormented the entire trip was out there. The kid, sneaky and had to be seeking revenge for the crap I pulled on him, lurked about. I sat in shelter pondering my next move.

The owner barged into my solace, "you said the others were coming yesterday. If they ain't here tonight, I gotta run you out. This ain't no hotel I'm running. You're still a fugitive and the longer you stay here, the better chance I'll get caught. Holing up wanted men is a crime too. I ain't saving your ass over mine."

I didn't trust a soul. His statement sounded like a threat if I sheltered there for much longer. The man stormed out and left the same way he barged in. Overthinking the situation controlled my thoughts.

Sundown crept up on the village while I snuck out of shelter and on my own. I became more comfortable in the open day or night-time. I could shoot with the best, and could outride anyone, even with Kat on back gripping my belly.

I checked my gear, finding everything, and led the horse out of the barn. My ride and I slipped back in the direction we came from. I needed Kat sitting behind me, clinging to my stomach, and I had to succumb to Josiah's intelligence.

Keeping my horse trotting, while on the lookout for signs of a wagon hauling Uncle Zeke's property, I rode east. Plus, there was Clete scoping the area. I never trusted the kid, and that lack of trust could get us in trouble.

On catching sight of some fresh ruts left by wagon wheels, I vanished south into the forest while I left my little cousin as reptile bait. The upcoming scenarios overplayed in my head. I no longer cared about Josiah and Millie, but prayed they'd made it. Right now, I only wanted Kat. I would grab her and run to the border with no cousins along. Josiah and Millie slowed me down.

My horse let out indignant snots, expressing his displeasure of the trot and its desire for sprints. The clearing was an open straight path to the gulf. Kicking my boy's sides with my boots, we took off at a speed that left me clinging for life. The trees cleared out and the scent of sea water took over my senses and fifteen minutes later we took a break to let my steed lap up some stream water. With fresh fruit abundant, he grabbed pears off low-hanging trees.

The scent of the gulf grew stronger as I continued to ride. The horse and I rested behind one of the last three lines before the sand. We needed water and fruit, and I found no sign of my cousins or the women. The trail of the wagon wheels continued until the mud turned to sand. The wind had picked up, tossing the sand. I lost the trail; however, I continued riding Southwest-the required direction.

My first view of the ocean was the waves splashing onto the sand and continued to do so while the backwash ripped the soil into the gulf. I led the horse to the water's edge, riding through the splashes, admiring the shells along the way. Dried up crustaceans, jellyfish and other sea creatures lay abandoned on the shore.

The sun had begun its descent, so I hurried the stallion. I glanced around and noticed the rut dug in the muddy upper bank near the forest. Stopping to observe the furrows as they dug into the thicket, I wondered if this was my group and if

Cletus was with them. I had to be careful. Not sure if any Rangers or posse was searching for me this far away. I drew the horse to a halt, listening for human or non-human noises. I heard nothing but the waves splashing on the sand behind me and the wind blowing through the swampland near the gulf.

Further into the marsh, we crept away from the gators floating while the wagon grooves vanished.

"Ah." A scream from further into the swamp. "Robert." A male voice, possibly Josiah's.

"Robert." The shriek came from a younger female voice that I recognized as Kat's, even though the scream was distant.

"Kat, Josiah, Millie. Where are you?" I screamed into the marsh.

The singing was louder than the hollering. Both gals sang in harmony, like a choir. The tune echoed through the grove and into my head.

"Well now, if you get there before I do

Comin' for to carry me home

Tell all my friends that I'm a-comin' too

Comin' for to carry me home"

I was sure it was them *but* couldn't put an eye on them. I made to reach for my field glasses, but soon ignored the thought. Any distraction could cost my life. I rode towards the bay, rifle in hand, a finger short of squeezing the trigger of the pistol and ready to fire.

The shrieks continued, as did the singing. The landmark was becoming familiar as I crept west toward the tip of the bay. I noticed the upper tips of a mast and the head of the sail and sensed a moderate sized ship nearby.

My father and the man in Beaumont had both told me that this was a major trafficking area for Africans. Pirates also roamed the Gulf of Mexico. Sweat dripped from my hat since the brim became soaked. My hands and legs trembled, while my heartbeat like an old man's. With Josiah and Kat's screams, whoever had them knew I approached.

The horse and I snuck further in, waiting for another verse or holler. I could only see the sail and mast. I wondered if they were on the ship or hiding in the swamps. Riding forward, I saw the full- scale ship. The boat sat in the bay, not more than twenty yards from landfall and not exactly horizontal or vertical. The boat tipped into the water at a slight angle. Unable to hear my crew and with no clue where they hid, my suspicious nature took over. Did I even hear them? Or did I hear the ghosts of slaves on a hijacked ship? I proceeded with caution. My horse sniffed the vegetation along the way until it parted and turned into sand.

"Robert," Kat shrieked. Her tiny legs and body came shooting out of the swamp. "Robert, I'm glad you are here." The force of her hug knocked me on my bottom. "Mil, Josiah and Cletus are here."

"Is it a trap? Is Josiah in on it?"

"Robert, I don't know if he is. Cletus found us and brought us here." She paced the grounds in circles, twiddling her thumbs.

"Right now, I trust you and me, but my instinct gets me in trouble. I don't even trust myself right now." I grabbed her hand and led her towards the ship. "What about Mil? Is she safe?"

"I'm not sure about any of them. Scavengers trapped us. The old man, Mil, Josiah and Clete."

"They let you run?"

"Yeah, I just ran when I knew it was you."

"It's a trap. Hop on." We mounted the pony and rode off into a thicket, not knowing who or what was waiting. For now, I cared less about my cousins. Getting Kat and me to freedom was all that mattered.

"Robert? What about the ship?" Kat asked. I halted the steed.

"Scalawags on it, I'm sure."

"I think we can take it towards the next land, get another forty miles further down. Put some distance between the two."

I did not know how to sail a ship, and I bet she didn't either. I trusted her, so I gave her a knife and pistol. We galloped back to the ship, this time slowing down in front, looking for any sign of life. No sign of Mil and my cousins. We would venture out alone if needed.

The ship was bent over, but appeared not to take water in. We would not take it to Mexico, just a couple of islands further down the coast. The only boats I ever steered were skiffs on the Sabine, Red, and Cane Rivers. A schooner like this will take some figuring out. The wind direction and sails I could handle, and all we needed was to get to a couple of ports away. Now I needed to know if the ark was vacant.

I barged onto the watercraft, Kat on my tail. Knife in one hand, pistol in the other, with Kat right behind, also armed with similar weapons. We mimicked the seagulls circling the ship as we surrounded the inside of the schooner in search of crew or pirates who captured the watercraft, dead prisoners or survivors laying in the hatch. The wood creaked as we paced across it and jiggled with every step. Gulls attacked, also searching for the raw flesh of survivors.

Twenty minutes into our search that turned up nothing after busting open different cabins, we assumed we were the sole passengers on board. We climbed a ladder back to the main deck, inching towards the front of the vessel. The wood cracked in front of me, and I tripped. Kat was close behind and, though she didn't anticipate my stumble, she never lost focus and took more steps.

She fell through the crevice I created all the way to the bottom. Her screams followed her down, prompting me to turn and fall towards her. The stench reminded me of back in 54 when Pa's pigs all caught cholera. Kat puked on the objects. I was afraid to look, but my duty was to take care of her.

After she vomited a third time, I reached her and pushed her away from the pungent stench. The adjacent room was too far away, but I lifted her up and carried her until the smell dissipated. I sat her down and attempted a rapid investigation. An abandoned and hijacked slave ship in the bay. Being abandoned in a sinking ship was their burial. The boat was still afloat, and on a quick look was still navigable.

After puking twice, I studied the corpses quickly. Slaves, dead property who never made a profit for the sellers, and never worked for the likes of Uncle Zeke. These people were the lucky ones, and I had a brand-new perspective. The deceased were on a suicide mission and their spirits will help us.

I crawled through to where I left Kat, and we crawled back up through the cabin and onto the main deck.

"Were they who I thought they are?" She looked at me, eyes red, tears dropping.

"Yep." I felt as bad as she did.

"Their spirits will guide us to shelter." She attempted a smile and stood up, proceeding to walk to the mast. The sails needed adjusted. "This way they didn't die in vain."

Kat and I thought alike. She picked the right cousin, and I eyed the right girl when it was bath time for the families.

We surveyed the sails. They seemed intact. All we needed to do was adjust them. The wind picked up from the southeast. We'd be floating straight into the breeze if we wanted to stay close to the sound. We've made it this far, improvising.

In the distance a cart rode towards us, led by an old black man and Mil rode next to him. No sign of Josiah and I wondered if Cletus was with him. Three horses led the buggy, and I assumed my younger cousin was traveling. I didn't care since there was a plank. If Clete got out of hand, he could go swimming. He grew up a river rat, so the boy knew how.

We searched for the anchor rope as they rode up on the wagon, crossing in the shallow part of the bay where we sat. Kat and I observed them board the boat. Mil led the way, followed by both my cousins. Josiah and Clete walked beside each other, and the youngest walked free with no shackles or cuffs. The old man stayed back with the wagon.

"Ain't, you crossing with us?" I asked him.

"I gotta get back. Mastah, be looking for me." He turned his head as if expecting someone.

"Ain't no one looking for you now, is there?" His neck-twisting raised my paranoia.

"Son, when you a negro, everyone looking for you. When you a fugitive stealing negroes, everyone looking for you, too. I needs to get back."

"Take this cracker back with ya." I put a chokehold on Cletus. I wanted him at knifepoint but decided against poking him with the blade.

The old man hollered across the swamp. "That boy gonna bail you out somewhere on this trip. Spirits say so, and da spirits are strong on this boat."

Clete held his nose once he whiffed the stench.

I released my cousin as the rest waved goodbye to the elder statesman. We continued to work on straightening the mast to get the sails upright. The plan was to make it a couple of ports away or as far as the partially damaged ship took us. I sliced the anchor rope, so that the anchor free-fell into the depths of the bay. Josiah and his brother continued adjusting the mast with the help of the girls.

They loosened the sails from the main mast. The girls searched their rucksacks for items that could assist in mending the loosened sail. Objects ricocheted on the rickety deck as they searched deeper into their bags. Josiah wandered around the fallen mast, leaving me sitting all confused and wondering how this thing would set sail.

Josiah scratched his chin with his index finger. He stared at the fallen log attached to the cloth, moseyed to the sail and peeked at the rope. He gave it a firm tug. "Robert, this strand of rope is loose." He yanked on it again and it came through the pulley. "Thread this through the pulley while I check the rest. It should be all we need to raise the sails. Mil and Kat can mend these sails up a bit."

Josiah scooted across the rickety floor. Squeaks came from the floor of the ship as he stumbled across broken flanks. He found another loose rope and pulley and hollered for me to fix this one when he finished. I'm not sure why he didn't ask his younger brother, but my mistrust of Cletus must be contagious. Clete sat in the corner taking everything in, watching in solitude as us four worked as a team. I wanted to get moving and make him walk the plank.

The girls wandered the top of the ship searching for anything cloth like so they could repair lacerations on the sails.

"I'm going to the lower level." Mille told her friend as she proceeded to the steps, stumbling on the flimsy floor.

"You want me to come down too?"

"No, "she snapped. "I don't want you to see what's down there."

Kat looked at her unafraid. "There are bodies down there." She rose and approached her friend, but Millie proceeded down the steps as if dragged by spirits. Kat hesitated like she felt something and ran to where I threaded the rope through the pulley. I worked it to the bow to tie the knot. I tugged and it felt tight, tight enough to hoist the sail once it got patched.

Josiah stumbled in my direction to check the knot and rope. "Damnit, that ain't close, Robert. One good wind gust and that knot will be undone. Can't you feel the gulf breeze?" His eyes rolled to the top of his head as he stomped where Mil would arrive, swearing under his breath. I worked harder but kept an eye on my cousin and his gal.

Mil returned to the deck. She crawled up and knelt at her man's feet. She appeared nauseous with her head bent over. I thought she was going to regurgitate on my cousin's toes. He grabbed her hands and pulled her up, his arms around her. I continued watching them, still twiddling with the rope. She whispered something to Josiah as he squeezed her closer.

I stopped working. Kat scooted towards them, and I joined them by the steps. Millie had news, and I had to know what was up. The thought of dead slaves in the stern of the ship repulsed yet intrigued me enough to create new ideas in my head, The thought of open sailing down the gulf and into Mexico, or just around population intrigued me, it would make our escape to freedom smooth sailing.

I approached the three and met with an angry glare. Josiah turned to me screaming. "I assume the rope is tied; the pulleys are working on all sides. If not get your scrawny ass back and get working!" He turned back to Mil and grabbed the pieces of cloth she carried upstairs still hollering at me. "She cut this cloth from around dead slaves' peckers, and you can't tighten knots all the way. Who should we let take charge? Not you!"

I wanted to fight Josiah, but it would be counterproductive. I glanced around the deck and saw the satisfied glint lit Clete's eyes. He relished the division. Once there was a crack, it was easier to divide. I needed to swallow my pride, and work with him, but I saw the dissolution of my cousin's relationship. Getting Kat and I across the gulf and towards freedom was my focus, with or without my cousins, and by any means necessary.

Kat and Millie used their makeshift sewing kits to attach the loincloths from the former slaves to the sails. They may have sabotaged their ship, but the folks would not die in vain. I worked harder in getting the ropes ready. Josiah tested them and felt they were finally okay.

"About time." The sarcastic tone remained in his voice. "All five of us need to raise the masts." He called the girls and his younger brother over. It was the first time Josiah's opportunist little brother assisted. Once the sails were set, he retreated again to the corner to watch his brother and I carefully, but kept an eye on Kat, waiting to take advantage. We all hoped and prayed to whatever god may be listening that the boat would sail. As of now we remained near the islands and would revert to plan A if the ship began taking in water.

With the sails set, and both Josiah and I taking the rudder alongside the other three in proximity, we set sail.

Josiah and I struggled to command the ship. We both wanted to wear the captain's hat, however neither of us knew what we were doing. The boat drifted away from land and further than I wanted. Josiah felt confident in his navigation skills. I didn't, nor did I have confidence in the vessel.

"Sit down, Robert."

I kicked back and stretched out, relaxing a bit. I conceded leadership for the time being.

Josiah continued, "I've always wanted to do this. Sail, sail away from all the shit my father put us through."

"You never told me" I watched him take the wheel, and I reluctantly let him steer while forgiving his demanding actions earlier. People act different when stressed and hijacking a ship that had crashed near Galveston Island certainly seemed exasperating. The vessel headed out into the choppy gulf waters, bouncing along the way. Ceding control to my oldest cousin, I closed my eyes to catch a brief nap, letting the watercraft rock me like my mother would a small child.

I awoke a short time later to Kat's frizzy hair on my bare chest with soft breaths escaping her half-open mouth. I could see above the ship. I searched around, looking for the Texas gulf, but still needed the shore to remain in sight. I didn't trust the boat or the sailor to keep this afloat as long as we needed it to, plus there was a potential hijacker on board. Clete knew his place. The kid was a patient, contemplative boy who laid back, waiting to strike. I nudged Kat off my chest, reached for my field glasses which laid by my dirty ripped shirt, and I staggered closer to Josiah.

The glasses were raised. Peeking around through the lens confirmed the shore no longer was within sight. I figured that confronting my cousin at this time wasn't an option, since I wanted to keep the shore in sight. Josiah, after handling the boat, had other ideas as we bounced further and further into the gulf. He flipped his long blonde locks back over his shoulder. The look of a possessed man took over as he steered to lead us straight to Mexico by boat.

Either we were on a suicide mission, or he had some spiritual inside information, which is what I became afraid of. I could control how far out we sailed, however causing a mutiny wasn't in my nature. Not yet anyway, but Josiah continued to flash the crooked smile and look down at me, knowing who remained captain. The smug arrogance he had never shown before stripped the personality I was used to. Was he this way all along? Right then, I made up my mind to take over the ship, but when?

Chapter 14

We drifted away from the coast. I didn't like sailing into the unknown with a cousin, whose only idea of what he was doing came from dreaming about being a Navy Commander as a kid. As he matured and woke up to the evils of his father and those sharing his thinking in the south and north, he no longer wanted to sail. I couldn't tell if he absorbed from an early reading, if he read books on navigation, or whether it only a dream. Just like my dream was to be a master soldier fighting for the nation. I was on my way.

As the land faded from view, I returned to him. Curiosity reeked from my soul. "What happened anyway? You took two days to get here, and why does Clete keep showing up?"

Josiah fiddled with the wheel, and from the look of things was stirring the ship closer to shore. He peered into my eyes without blinking. The Gulf breeze refreshed me as water splashed into the boat, but the winds and the sails continued to sit perfectly, cruising us deeper into the gulf.

"The old man, the ship, Mil, and my little brother, all had to be there. I don't know why. Mil explained it to me, but it was all spiritual crap. You know how father raised me, thinking it was God's plan to own the girls," Josiah said. He pointed towards Kat and Mil.

"I don't understand either. Then again, I don't understand Jesus and his teachings. How does he heal the sick, I mean, how the hell did all this happen? Pa said trust him and it will happen. Maybe we have to trust this God, instead of the one we were raised to put our faith in."

"Well, to answer your question, the old man, Mil, Kat and I spent some time in the open field. He was free to come and go, and his Master, a good man, gave us a pass. We sat out last night under the blood moon and talked. Well, Mil and him did. They think they're long-lost kin, you know?"

"I heard that about them. What about Kat? She came up from this area?"

"She don't even know. I feel bad for her. Can you imagine not having a clue where your kin came from?"

"At least we know we came from Acadia. I'm still not sure how both our Pas think so different."

"Cause my Pa kissed granddaddy's ass, that's why. Your Pops woke up and educated himself about the world."

"Yeah, he knew we were at war, and when we weren't at war, we stole from Indians and Mexicans, ravaging everything in their path, including the women. He would have preferred that we own a little plot of land next to the Caddo and fish to farm like them and live with them assimilating cultures."

"Exactly why Gramps gave your pa a measly acre across Caddo territory from us. He was cross at such thinking and appalled that his own son would consider such an idea."

"So, we need Clete on this?" I asked. "Maybe I shouldn't have tried to dump him off for gator bait so many times."

"I can't blame ya. I wanted him gone too, but he's my brother is one reason, and talking to the old man, he's not only needed but required to come with us."

"But why?"

The wind gained momentum. Josiah inhaled the stench from below and his fingertips squeezed his nostrils shut. A reddish glow shot from his eyes, transforming his smile into a sneer. "Sacrificial lamb. I need some alone time with Mil. Here, steer this. I'll send Kat over to join you."

He showed me how to guide the sails. I wanted to keep it closer to shore, but we were making good time and the boat seemed to hold water. Kat joined me as darkness fell over the gulf. We had no maps to guide our journey except the spirits below, the sun, and the moon and stars.

"I trust you. Is all this true about the spirits?" I asked.

We sat near the rudder from where we controlled the vessel. The sun was setting ahead of us by the time we made headway in a westerly direction.

She replied, "I'm not sure, Robert. Mil and that ol' man seem to think so. You gotta learn to trust yourself as well as others including God, and God controls the spirits of those above and the spirits of those below the deck. Trust Josiah, Mil, and even Clete and, of course, me."

"You know our entire plans have changed. Perhaps I never had any strategy this entire time. I just wanted to run away with you and start a life together somewhere." I scanned across the water. The gulf was fascinating as waves cascaded against the ship. "I'm still making it up."

"You're not making this up now. Your failing to follow the spirit separated us but following them brought us together. Now, we are sailing to freedom."

"This boat ain't gonna make Mexico. We'll be lucky if it makes land."

"Robert!" she snapped. "If you trust those bodies below, you won't talk like that. We're gonna make landfall. Those dead bodies also want us. The old man said they want runaways to make it to freedom."

"Do you know why Cletus is with us? Josiah looked like the devil when I asked him. His eyes turned red, and his smile lay crooked. I swore flames shot out his ears."

"Robert, ain't your daddy a preacher? Trust the plan. Moses trusted the plan. It works the same way. You a lot like Moses cause you set my family free and now you setting me and Mil free. You don't know you following a plan, but God is leading you, Robert. Trust him and stop asking questions."

Pa had told me the story about a billion times, but I never found the relevance until now, and even at Kat's brief tutoring as we sailed. I could not see the comparison between me and some old prophet from biblical days.

"How old is your father? Ain't he about forty?" she asked. Kat's questions made me feel like I had the right partner, and she might be too good for me.

"He just turned forty-one," I told her.

"When Moses first went to Israel to set the people free, he was just forty. Took him a lifetime to do it, but you are starting now. You might have set me and Mil and our families free, but there are a bunch of us who ain't free. Setting us all free will take generations."

I felt guilty for stealing her. Zeke's other slaves were good people. I was sure some were valiant members of their native tribes, who fell into trapper's hands in their native land. I felt selfish but getting Kat and Millie out with their families was my goal. The boat rocked in the gulf waters, aligning with her hands which stroked my bicep. I smiled as she moved closer to kiss me. The kiss lasted longer and was more passionate than others.

When our lips separated, she cooed. "You are him. Moses, just like my father. That's why I wanted you to take me, and when I caught you peaking at me bathing, I didn't try covering nothin."

Until this moment, I didn't know she knew I stole quick glances of her in the tub, but Kat reassured me throughout the night, we did the right thing.

We drifted through the gulf. I'm not sure how one releases control to God, or The Devil or anyone. Pa raised me to be self-sufficient and to depend on my strengths to lead me. We floated throughout the night on a questionable boat. There was the unbearable stench of rotting, decaying dead bodies inside the deck of the ship, a traitorous cousin on board to combat with, and I've never captained a ship in my life. Josiah may have read books, and fantasized about it earlier in his life, but that is not experience. I wanted to trust any God.

Kat and I steered the ship and ate some jerky we saved. Mil and Josiah disappeared to a remote area of the ship for their extended private time. Left to his own devices, Cletus wandered about. What he was doing, no one knew, and his actions were key to our plans. Someone would set up a trap after landfall somewhere. That's all I knew. I pondered the God given signs.

I figured Josiah would come back and steer the watercraft, but I was wrong. He never returned that night. It was up to me. Maybe there was a spiritual reason it was left for me to guide the boat, at the mercy of the forces of nature to keep the vessel in the right direction. I used the stars and wind to guide us, but Kat's soothing touch relaxed me. As long as the wind didn't change directions, we were good as the ship drifted southwest.

Josiah never returned that night. We spotted Cletus making mad dashes across the deck like a little kid running amuck. Kat relaxed at my feet. Slight snores escaped her body as she drifted in and out of sleep, lured by the boat bouncing in the gulf. I stirred the ship closer, doing my best to adjust the sails. What I didn't want to happen is to steer the boat further out than we were.

The thought that we were being guided by the spirits of dead slaves on the bottom of an abandoned ship didn't give me much confidence. Then again, I wanted control. Relinquishing it to corpses was beyond my belief. After a few nudges on the rudder and a twist on the mast, I tweaked the boat in a more westward direction. Once spun, I stretched out next to my girl and held her. I trusted her guidance for our arrival in Mexico.

We woke with the sun rising behind us and my cousins nowhere to be found. Kat excused herself for some morning hygienic duties, giving me the chance to dash off to do the same. The Texas heat and sun did wonders on us. Diving in the blue salt water of the Gulf was tempting but getting back on board would pose great difficulty.

I grabbed the field glasses and sprinted to the bow. All I saw for a long stretch was water everywhere, no land in sight as I squinted into the glasses. Being lost at sea was something I didn't want; however, I enjoyed the freedom of not having to look over my shoulder or wonder if the next person I noticed would shoot me down, capture me for reward money and haul the girls back with Josiah in chains. In all this, at the end Clete would be lauded as a hero.

The water of the gulf was like glass, waves were nonexistent. I rushed back to the wheel to find Josiah sitting with Millie, twisting the sails in the other direction from the previous night.

"What did you do last night? I'm steering this according to the ghosts below." His voice was confrontational. He clenched his fists and threw his arms in the air.

"I don't want to go further out. I doubt if this thing will go much further. One of us needs to check the deck, make sure it's not leaking."

"You two should go down. It's our turn to steer. Check everything out."

"Josiah," Kat said. "Last time I went down, I vomited all over. That stench got to me."

Millie spoke up. "That stench is leading us to freedom. We need them dead bodies here. Remember, Kat, they died so we can make it. Putting up with the aroma is our sacrifice."

"What if this thing sinks? We're seeking freedom, not to be lambs to the spirits."

"Go down below and check for leaks!" Josiah screamed. Kat scowled at him.

"Don't shout..." Kat tried fighting back.

Josiah lifted his hand to halt the fight. When he was at the wheel, he was in charge. I still wondered what happened to Cletus. Instead of arguing with the captain, I decided to explore the ship. Further answers could only come with a little investigative work.

I grabbed Kat's hand and pulled her through the vessel like we did on our initial exploration. I lit a torch to aid us in the dark. Leaks wouldn't appear magically if we couldn't see them. We got to the bottom of the maritime and initiated the search. Droplets of water appeared on the hull, but nothing extraordinary. We both took note.

We proceeded towards the corpses and stench. Treading our way through the bottom of the ship with fingers holding tight out noses, the stink of the corpses knocked us down so that we crawled on all fours. I saw Cletus on all fours in prayer position saying ineligibles to the carcasses. I wondered if he sold his soul, or if he discovered his role in this.

Kat was heaving as if she needed to regurgitate. Her eyes met mine, noticing my cousin's actions. He seemed to be in a trance. I watched my younger cousin and whatever soul he had left in his fourteen-year-old self-body absorbed into the stink. He continued kneeling. I wondered if his motionless body was among the living. I proceeded forward a step, but Kat lifted her hand to halt me. She pointed back in the direction we came from.

Sneaking out of the polluted area, we noticed the water. I wanted to check if more liquid from the gulf entered the bottom. Puddles already replaced the drops. The ship was taking in water. We hurried above deck to let Captain Josiah aware of the situation.

I rushed up the steps with Kat on my heels. Each step on the boat up to the deck seemed to creek. At the last one Kat fell through as she tumbled on them. Drops of crimson dripped from her shins as she struggled to get free. I grabbed her hand, tugging her to her feet, and then we finished our jaunt.

"Water is leaking in. The steps are giving way. We need to get this thing ashore now." My breath was uneven due to my voice shaking. I wasn't sure how quick the boat would sink, but it was falling apart.

Josiah glanced at me; his eyes still portrayed a devilish glow. "That's not the plan, Robert." He failed to adjust the sails.

"Josiah," Kat interjected. "We will not make it on this boat. I heard the stories about our ancestors going down. We'd rather be dead than slaves, but this is us right now. We're on a mission for survival, not death. Turn the ship, or we will."

Josiah looked at me, Kat, and then at Millie. The old man's stories must have gotten to him. "Help me, Robert," he said with reluctance. "Let's get this pointed towards shore. With any luck we will be far enough South. The old man said once we get to the Southern part of Texas, we'll have more help. Mexicans hate the white man as much as the slaves, plus lots of freed blacks hanging out."

"You know I don't trust anyone so, I ain't taking no help."

"We still got the spirits."

"The spirits were taking us down," Kat spoke up again. "They wanted us to go with them."

All five of us began tugging on the ropes. The sails moved to steer the boat in a westerly direction. With the field glasses rested on my nose, I searched for land; however, it was still too early. I no longer trusted my cousin. I had to be sure we were headed for land.

Kat and I headed to the front of the vessel. We alternated scouting towards land, but after hours of scanning the horizon, the coast still evaded us. We rushed back to Josiah, his traitorous little brother, and Millie.

"You sure we are going the right direction?" Kat asked, taking charge of the situation.

We got the sails adjusted. "We need all the divine intervention we can get. I don't care what side it's from," Josiah said.

"How about we ride like holy hell until we make landfall and figure out where we're at?" I took control of the ship, with Kat at my side. I knew the two of us would make it but wondered about my cousins and Millie.

The boat was on a pattern straight to coast. I had no idea where, but after a few hours of sailing, Millie came sprinting back. "Land ahead, land ahead," she screamed with Josiah hot on her heels.

"Little cousin, we're making great time. I'm going down to check on Clete and the leaks. Keep running straight."

Millie stayed with us the whole time he dashed off. Kat and Millie sat next to each other; legs crossed, while I did my best to keep the ship straight. Land was still not visible with the naked eye. I did not know how long it would take until landfall. Stranded on a barrier island was better than being shark bait if we sank to the bottom of the gulf with spirit producing corpses.

Millie peeked at me. "Robert, are we gonna make it? I wish that ol' man didn't talk to Josiah about spirits. We were just careful. I'm afraid we ain't gonna make shore. Seems like we are slowing down."

Kat scooted over and put her arm around her friend to comfort her. She smiled as I took charge, admiring my confident look. Inside, I shook since I was as petrified as everyone else.

"Robert is taking over now. He's sure we can make it to land. Let's sit back, get something to eat, and relax. We should be good. We just need to pray to da spirits to get us safe on land."

"Which spirits we praying to?" Millie asked.

Kat had no answer. She peered at me to guide her response. Being the son of a preacher, she knew I had the answer.

I sat in front of them, knees drawn up with arms around my joints. Swallowing before speaking, I said, "Pray, just pray to whichever God you think will get us here. Jesus will forgive you if you welcome him back into your life. The corpses down below want us to make it. They don't want to have died in vain." I peered at both lasses. "Who do you feel strongest about?"

Millie spoke, but Kat put out a hand to hush her. "Robert, don't want to know who you feel strongest about. He wants you to pray to whichever God has your interest. Is that right?"

"That's right, just pray."

We bowed our heads, eyes closed, we said our silent prayers. Once finished, I walked over to where I would get a glimpse of the shore. Kat followed me, leaving Mil alone since Josiah and his brother still hadn't returned.

We strolled to the front, out on the bow spirit, all the while clinging to whatever we could. The ship was traveling with the wind and waves. It wasn't as bumpy as it could have been. I pulled the glasses to my eye again and spotted land. It was still in the distance, not visible without field glasses, but seeing the shores even at a distance made my breaths come easier. We eased our way back to the deck and stopped.

"We gonna make it?" Kat asked.

I caressed her pretty face, pulled her close, and kissed her lips. "Did that answer your question?" I smiled.

We returned across the rickety deck, hand in hand to find drama.

Josiah and Clete stood arguing. The older brother had a knife to his younger brother's throat. Cletus sat next to Millie.

"Drop it, Josiah!" I shouted. "We're close to land, and I feel this ship slowing up. We need to be all be on the same side."

"He was trying to rape Millie."

"That's her purpose. I did her before on the plantation before you got her. I wanted to get her again. She's still property." The kid smirked at me. "I got to Kat before you, too. Daddy's property, remember? You going to kill me now? Make me walk the plank?"

I wanted to, but I needed every vibration to be right. Peace had to be with us. Water infiltrated the bottom, reducing the ship's speed.

"Both of you head to the front and search for land. No one is going overboard. The three of us will steer this thing into land."

Chapter 15

We packed everything on the three horses right before we struck bottom. The waves of the blue water splashed onto the boat as we rode our horses through the gulf. The light sand was a mere acre away, while the ride should be quick to get onshore. I had to get off that boat at all costs. I was a horseman, not a sailor. The sun started its descent as my horse splashed into the gulf waters. Kat clung tight to my belly, while my two cousins trailed behind. We rested the horses after getting a few days' break from riding. We were tired since the spiritual ride on the abandoned merchant ship took its toll. I wasn't sure where we were, but Mexico was down the shore. I had no idea how far, and if we could ride the outer banks down. There was nobody on them, so I sped up once the horse rid through sand. I wanted an all-night ride until we found a trader, trapper or anyone who could tell us where we were.

Later that evening our speed dissipated. The damp sand was good for the hooves of the horses, but even the well-rested stallions didn't feel like galloping. Right now, they needed saved for when speed was a necessity. We trotted for a few more miles before a glimmer of light reflected off the gulf from the moon. I could see well enough to make a small camp. We undid the bedrolls and all five of us took a deserved nap. The next day might be different.

We nestled up on the beach, the two couples separated with Clete about half-way in between. I had no plans, since we were more than halfway to freedom, and I got us this far. The sun rose behind us over the gulf. We woke to gather food, build a fire and hunt for fish and some food. The ladies stayed hidden to build the fire, while I carved a spear out of wood, in hope some fish wandered too close to the shore.

Josiah and his younger brother wandered the forest in search of fresh berries. The five of us needed nourished. We were tired of jerky. I searched the other side of the beach, the inlet narrow, and it looked crossable on horseback. I waded out into the merk, spear in hand, hoping to jab a meal. Meanwhile, I was interested in the land on the other side of the inlet. Land stretched out to the edge. I recognized the plant. Cotton. We were adjacent to a plantation and Texas hadn't abolished slavery either. This was the best place to cross, however a night crossing was required. I needed to scout it out and figure out where we were.

"IS THIS WHERE CLETE WILL BE SACRIFICED?"

The thought wasn't mine. I smiled at the idea. How would we use him? I had wondered about the idea since he boarded the ship, at the time Josiah grinned like the devil at me. Clete will help us but will eventually get caught. I spotted a red snapper. With full rage, I took out my frustration on the fish and caught us a meal. This land needed explored.

I hiked back with the fish, stabbed and gutted out. Five of us sat down and had a decent meal, after which I plotted to set up the youngest of the group. It might happen on the plantation across the inlet, or maybe the next one down. As usual, I'd use my gut instead of my brain. No one said this would be easy, casualties or prisoners needed taken. He wanted to join; his purpose was not clear.

"I'm headed out across that plantation over there, since we need to do some scouting." I didn't want to ask Cletus, but if he volunteered, my plan would come together sooner than later. No response. "I'll be back by nightfall, and we can roll if things are clear. If not, we spend another day."

I needed to take charge. Josiah was too cerebral for a mad dash across a large state. I needed his brains for strategic moves, but his problem was he thought too much. He overthinks situations. However, I needed to involve him somehow.

"Josiah, once we get moving, we need a map. I think there are too many bays and inlets along the coast. I want to run straight and quick. It might be the plantation up here or the next. Can you do it?" I asked him.

"Yeah, you think there are slaves up here?"

I looked at him like he was a fool. My eyes rolled upwards, and I gave him a smirk. "This is Texas still. They are the same as back home. We still must protect the girls. I'm not sure if we're wanted this far out or not." I looked at Cletus. He didn't look back.

I rode my horse across the swamp, pulling up on the plantation, at first at a trot, checking out the land. It was the back end of a cotton field, nothing special. The quarters for the owner's property set up the road field. I trampled the profits of the back of his land.

Nothing out of the ordinary. In the distance, I saw the labor flipping the fluffy flowers into sacks. However, everyone kept their distance. I rode on. I rode near the water, keeping as far away from the owner's homes as possible with still no sign of life anywhere except wide fields. I rode for two hours, making fifteen miles and nothing. I turned the horse around and returned to our camp. We'd ride off in the morning.

The next morning was the same. I caught fish, fruit picked, the fire burned low as we remained hidden in the marsh. Swamp creatures ignored us. They knew we were dangerous if they attacked and harmless if they left us alone. We were one with the reptiles.

Soon enough, we were riding off again. We passed the same spot I rode to the previous day. There was no sign of people, only vast fields lay ahead as we rode forward. Kat clung to my chest, head covered, disguising her race. Millie did the same with Josiah. From a distance, we appeared as one rider unnoticed.

Two days and nights passed as we raced around the bays and inlets of the gulf coast. As far as I knew we went unnoticed, however, when we slowed to a trot, we saw slave labor working the fields. The longer we rode, the further from the coast we were. The vegetation changed a little as the thicker forests diminished. Grasslands took control. Hiding places dwindled.

I halted my horse with Kat still clinging to my stomach. We waited for the others to catch up, so that we rested atop a minor bluff with a remote village sitting in the valley. I focused the field glasses on the community, which gave Kat space to relax her grip on my gut. I let her dismount to stretch, so that I could use the opportunity to check the village and the surrounding areas.

My cousins arrived, and everyone dismounted. Everyone wanted to stretch their arms and legs and stroll around.

"IT'S TIME."

Josiah glanced at me as if he heard the voice. It was time to say goodbye to his brother. He bowed his head in prayer and went to give him a hug.

"GOODBYE, MY BROTHER."

It wasn't cousin's voice; it was deeper, with more dialect of an older slave, perhaps a descendant from the ship, perhaps an unborn who never witnessed life, like his ancestors who worked the fields.

I glanced at my older cousin, wondering if he heard or even recognized the voice. He didn't acknowledge me but simply stepped away.

"Why are you hugging me?" Clete asked.

Josiah motioned for me to approach. Kat and I inched forward. "Can Mil fit behind Kat?"

"Yeah, not for a long ride, maybe out of sight, a few acres away."

"Stay here, Clete. Robert and I need to discuss something. I've come close to convincing him you're good and we need you. I need to discuss things in private."

The four of us disappeared into some brush outside the village.

. * * *

Josiah and Clete

A trading post sat on the corner across from three saloons. Tumbleweeds can be seen dancing across the dust streets. On this warn afternoon, Cletus and I entered the post with some furs, Robert and Kat trapped near the bay. Nothing fancy, just some raccoons and other smaller varmints. Not much that would earn train fare to the border but enough to know if we were wanted, and enough to set my cousin up for the theft of my father's property. It was enough money to create a diversion. At least that was what I thought.

The two of us scouted the store's exterior for any sign of wanted posters. They were all over East Texas. Would they have travelled this far South? If my guess was right, Clete spilled the beans on us. Father knew our destination, and Texas Rangers and Marshalls would search the state. Texas stretched up to the Indian Nations and South to Mexico. The territory of New Mexico laid to the west, but a world away. Our home was to the east in the adjacent state. We had been traveling forever.

I saw it first. A picture of Robert and Kat, slave and thief. Both wanted dead or alive. A poster of myself and Millie also plastered on an interior wall. Reward money listed that we had to be captured alive. The pictures of both of us were clean. I was clean shaven, my hair cropped short, but the picture was a month ago when we were at home after church.

A month later, there was no haircut, the whiskers disguised my face, smothered my chin, cheeks and neck. I was unrecognizable. My younger brother, whose whiskers never developed, looked like me. Our chins were similar.

Cletus stood around holding the pelts, while I strutted into the shop. I got the attention of the keeper, and a younger Caucasian man, who spoke with a European accent, possibly German.

"Can I help you, son?"

I wandered towards the wanted poster. The poster of me and Mil. I trusted Robert to keep the girls safe. I was glad he was with me. We wouldn't have made it anywhere close to this spot with his leadership and the spirits. I looked it over, ripping it from the window.

"Hey, son. Bring me the pelts."

Clete walked in and handed me some fur.

"Found this kid scavenging down by the gulf. What do ya think?"

I thought he was a dead ringer for me. The shopkeeper did too. He gave me the map, showed me the location, and typed on the telegraph. "I'd be more than happy to rope him up for ya."

The lasso Robert gave me and trained me on, I threw around his neck. One toss and I pulled it tight before I left. I took off on Clete's horse and sprinted to our hideout.

"Where's your brother?" asked Robert when I stopped.

"All roped up in the trading post. They got wanted posters of us. Damn little creep looked exactly like me. Shop owner was sending a telegram when I left. I got me a map. Let's check it out and get moving."

The shopkeeper pointed out we were in a village called Victoria.

Judging by the scale on the map he gave us, we were about 250 miles from the border. A five-day ride. We looked at each other after discussing the distance. "When do you want to take off?" Josiah asked me.

"Let's see what happens to Clete. I think we should be able to ride up, then take off at dusk."

We studied the map further in order to plot our route.

"Two days to this town down here by the bay."

"Pa said south of that, a ton of Mexicans roamed about who hate people like your father as much as Kat and Mil's family. We'll build up some allies for some smooth riding."

"Yeah, three of four days after that. Let's head up to town. I want to see the law dragging him before we ride off."

"I should have bopped him when I had my chances. There were too many."

"Glad you didn't. He showed his true colors. What are we going to do with his horse?"

"Someone in town certainly needs one." I looked at Kat, wondering if they wanted to ride, and if it would still be too risky. Her eyes were all over the stallion like she wanted ownership. I glanced at Josiah and back at Kat and Millie, who stripped Clete's bag from the saddle and tossed his gear on the ground in order to repack with their possessions.

"Reckon no one in town needs a horse." I helped them pack and mount the beast. Josiah went through his brother's gear. He picked up and read some papers and a diary.

"I'm glad we got rid of the traitor. You should have bopped him when you had your chance."

He showed me the passage. Clete scribed, "I WANTED TO STEAL BOTH GIRLS TO BE PART OF MY HAREM. I WANTED EAST TEXAS TO BE MINE, ONLY MINE, ONLY ME AND MY CHILDREN. THE LAND WOULD BE MY EMPIRE. THE GIRLS WERE PERFECT FOR BREEDING."

"He was setting us up."

"Was it the ship?" I asked my cousin.

"I think so. He didn't count on the spirits. Remember when he sat tranced by the corpses?"

"Yeah, he sat in silence, absorbing the stench which would make most of us vomit and feel like death."

"That was his sign of defeat. He knew his dreams of an empire were defeated."

"I wouldn't underestimate him. The kid is a sneak." Our eyes locked in agreement.

The four of us rode into town. The trading post was in the field glasses eyeshot. They tied several white horses up outside the post. Like we visioned, the younger brother of Josiah Barnum was drug out by men in white hats, the rope around his body, his body tied up. They rode in the opposite direction we headed as we spun the horses and headed towards Mexico. It would be a five-day journey.

Chapter 16

For the first two days we rode at night, blending in with the South Texas sky. The stars were the only light we saw as we snuck closer to our destination.

A stampede of wild horses woke us up to find hundreds of beasts roamed free, stampeding away from the village we hid in.

"Mustangs," I told the others as the horses continued their charge across the grassland.

"Where are they going?" Millie asked.

Josiah glanced at me, knowing I'm the horseman and expecting me to answer. I said nothing and let my cousin answer.

"They roam free, wild horses. I'm not sure where they're headed to besides the opposite direction we're headed."

I watched in amazement the thunderous roar of over a hundred sculpted equine. Our horses, quite aware, shook from the trees which held them. We dashed to stroke their head and murmured in soft voices. They continued kicking, heads shaking, and squealing so loud as though to let locals be aware of our presence.

"He won't settle down," Kat screamed, close to being kicked.

"Back away from him. Let him have his tantrum or you might get hurt." My steed knew me. I had ridden him for years. It was the same with Josiah. "Let me get him." I strolled over gently, not to alarm the animal. He was still in his outburst even as I approached.

I kept my voice low, relaxed, and calm. "It's okay," I tried to soothe. The squeals turned into whinnies, but he still bounced around, legs kicking, and was back to raising his fronts legs. Every time the horse went back to all fours, I crept closer, wanting to pat his forehead.

The Mustangs passed by the time the girl's horse eventually calmed down. We were ready to ride, despite that the horses still seemed excited. We stood close to them, packing them up with our gear.

"Don't move, senor." This command was followed by a quick click of a rifle.

Three Hispanic men with rifles pointed at the four of us.

I lifted my hands in surrender, as the others did.

"We got them," another Hispanic man said with an accent. He had a waybill with him, a poster that showed a sketch of us.

"We won't get no reward," the third seeming to be the leader spoke. "We hate the white man as much as the girls do. The boys stole them black girls. We need to help them."

I approached them. "You can help us to the border?"

"Si, Senor," the leader spoke.

"How far is it?" asked Josiah. He had lowered his hands as he approached.

"It's still two days away. Stick with us. There are lots of Texas Rangers around down here. They like to travel from here to the border. Runaways seem to relax when they get closer. Makes it easier picking for them."

Josiah poked me with the butt of his gun, and he grimaced. "We were about to ride in daylight. You saying we shouldn't?"

"I'm saying we can protect you." He pointed his rifle at a pear tree and squeezed the trigger. A pear dropped to the ground. He smiled at us and blasted more fruit.

I failed to trust anyone but the people I traveled with. I had my doubts about my cousin. Three Mexicans who came out of nowhere with rifles pointed at our heads now wanted me to trust them in a final two-day run to the border. They walked out from behind the brush, rifles aimed at us, cautiously inching forward.

Killing them was out of the question. I believed when they said they knew their way around the area. They had family and friends who expected them. If they came up missing, posses would be called.

We had a common enemy. The White man, who I was proud to be one. I had different beliefs and I'm sure Josiah and weren't alone, and only a minority of southern boys believed like we did. A brotherhood needed formed, and these men were now our brothers. If we were to live in Mexico, a new language and custom needed to be learned. I grabbed my knife and slashed my hand to allow drips of blood.

"Hermano," I told him, shaking his hand. I wanted to be one with them. I hoped for the same.

He glared at me, unaware of his next move. "Why did you cut your hand?"

"I want us to share blood and become blood brothers. We plan on living in Mexico there, and I want to learn your way of life."

"There is no need to cut your palm and spill your blood on me. This is honorable, and I acknowledge your request. We live here. We are citizens, and the Rangers still harass us.

I'm not afraid to kill. In fact, there are several dead lawmen at our hands."

We gathered up breakfast from what we could around the surrounding area, including pears and trapped varmints. After we doused the fire, we headed south, our minds lighter as we got closer to freedom. Riding like the wind, the leader of the trio and I led us closer to the border. Kat and Millie rode in the middle, Josiah and the other two trailed behind with guns ready to fire.

We kept close. I was ready to shoot if needed, the Mexicans we rode with were also ready, as well as Josiah. Kat controlled their horse. Millie had the rifle. Vegetation became scarce, bringing us to an opening where the soil was more made of sand dunes. There was nowhere to hide. The three Mexicans knew people who could escort us to the border. They called them the amigos of the riders, who specialized in aiding slaves to and across the border.

We stopped riding as soon as I noticed people on horseback in the distance. I set the rifle horizontal on the back of the horse so that it balanced on the equine. Through the field glasses, I noticed riders on about four horses.

"Are these the men we need to meet?"

My partner peered through his glasses. The tense air made the group on top of the dune move closer.

"My brothers nearby are small in number. There are only two of them." My Mexican partner said as he cocked his rifle. I heard the same from behind, as I made sure mine was ready to fire. Millie snapped her gun shut, too.

I nudged my chin at the man to my left, a signal that let him know he's in charge. We rode closer to each other, the girls sandwiched in between. Our horses trotted forward; I kept my glasses focused on the oncoming men as they started galloping.

"Texas Rangers," the man to my left said. He rode with his field glasses to his eye. "Bounty hunters are with them. Someone knew you were coming."

"Clete," I whispered so low that no one heard me.

I've never been in a gunfight. I felt unprepared as both sides turned into a gallop. The thought of shooting another human terrified me. I tugged on the rein in order to turn the horse westward. Josiah and the girls followed, while the Mexicans rode ahead to confront the ambush head on.

I tried to think up who could have set us up or was this the way it was going to be? These men were strangers and could have slaughtered us when they had a chance, or possibly they received payment to harvest runaway slaves. I got a good lead on everyone. From behind, I noticed Josiah and the girls lagging. I stopped, turned the horse around, and rode back. I needed Kat sitting behind me, hands wrapped around my gut. The horse sprinted back to where Josiah and the girls were.

"Get on," I yelled at Kat. "I want you with me."

Her face had a befuddled look, but she hopped off onto the ground. I dismounted and aided her onto mine. Millie took the reins, and they kept up the trot. Josiah stayed at the rear, guarding the back.

The land was still barren, no place to hide. We rode through the sand-based soil toward brush ahead and saw that a creek flowed freely. Not a perfect spot, however there was nothing else. We stopped to give the horses a drink and tie them up.

A lone rider came streaking through. Through the glasses, I saw a white man with a gun.

"We might have to take him," Josiah said, already in a kneeling position, gun pointed.

Kat stayed close to me. Millie pointed her weapon, and I aimed mine. The horses lapped water.

The rider arrived closer. I took a deep breath. Soon we would be in range and not well hidden. Millie crept further up front, her rifle continued aiming. As the man continued his approach, Millie raced from our shelter carrying the rifle, pointed at the rider. She was on a suicide mission to protect us from what might happen. He shot first. I heard the blast as Mil remained on foot. Josiah crept closer to his girl to protect her.

"I don't need you right now," she snapped at Josiah.

"I'm here to protect."

"I don't care if I live or die, Josiah. That's why I went on this mission. Being dead is better than being a slave. I'm tired of running. I was at peace with dat ol' man, but we running away again and people are shootin' at us."

Millie stood directly in front of the rider. She was so close that she could see the silver star he wore on his chest as a badge. His white hat flew off with the wind and speed he rode, floating down into the sand. He slowed to lift his revolver from the holster. Millie wanting to die, but also sought freedom, aimed. She squeezed the trigger. The ranger fell off the back of his steed and it dragged him through the soil until the rope broke. The horse continued its trot, leaving the man tumbled. Josiah ran towards him, past our terrible hideaway. He unloaded his revolver into the man for good measure.

Millie flopped on the ground, butt first. Josiah held the rest of her body upright, his arm around her shoulder. She pushed him away and ran off.

"I killed someone, and you shot six more holes in him to be sure. He wore a badge. We all are seeking a murder charge." She remained seated with her head between her knees. She continued, "I never shot a gun before and now I killed a man. I didn't want to kill him. I wanted to give myself up so you can run." Her voice broke in between sobs, until she rolled over in tears, face down, flooding the landscape.

"We need to skedaddle. Kat, can you help by riding with her? We're so close to freedom. One more day's ride. All of us will make I," I said.

Josiah abandoned Mil for the time, already mounted and trotting off towards the border. Millie, still in tears, accepted Kat's embrace. Kat raised her friend from the earth. They held hands back to the stolen horse that they both rode. Millie pulled herself up first, while Kat squatted in the saddle. I trotted behind then, keeping my eye out for a second ambush.

"Riders!" I yelled. Let's roll. I gouged my horse by the side, urging him to kick into high gear right away. Kat took off wanting to ride beside me, doing their best to catch up. Josiah's horse was the only steed, not at full sprint.

He continued wandering up, his horse in a trot. He'd already fallen behind. "Darling, come on." Millie's call prompted him to ride with more urgency.

"We shouldn't have killed the man. It should have been me who died."

He yelled across the prairie at his woman.

They rode up closer to me.

"I'd never let you die. I won't. If you die, I will too." He kicked the horse, forcing it into a gallop.

The landscape was changing. Most people we encountered were Mexicans with Caucasians sprinkled in. A group of Mexican were ahead of us pulling a wagon and other several on horseback. We rode to catch up and get in their caravan. Blending in was our best bet.

We rode with a large family of farmers into a market outside a village. Once inside, we could trade possessions with Hispanics who spoke English.

"How far is the border?" I asked.

The father of the group, a stout man wearing a sombrero and a plain long sleeve shirt glanced at Kat and Millie and smiled. He acknowledged the escape and theft. "It's about twenty miles away. Best place to cross is further west. Keep heading this same direction and you'll run into every slave catcher in the state." His accent thick, however, I understood the man.

"What about the law?" I asked.

He smiled again. "Law stays away from here. They don't last long."

It was getting late. We'd been riding all day and needed a place to bunk. "Any place to crash overnight?"

The man glanced over his shoulder, which made me cautious. Who was he looking for? Slave catchers, bounty hunters. Marshall's or Rangers? My instincts got us this far.

"What do you need, senor?" he asked.

"A place to hide overnight, and maybe an escort to the border, like we had coming in."

"Migrants come up and down from Mexico. Many live across the border and work up here for the ranchers. You ride down with them, stay inside the group. Gringo won't notice you."

"A good place to bunk?"

He looked around, continuing my suspicions of him. "Plenty of places you can hide." He didn't give a specific location. I felt comfortable.

The horses danced around the groves. Orange trees were thick, and we all felt it was a good place to hide out. Then again, if it was a good place for us to take shelter, slave catchers would hide in them too. I glanced at Kat; she's been my guiding light this trip.

"Where should we spend the night?"

She looked surprised since this was my job to lead and protect.

"Let's keep moving towards the border." Kat said.

I took the lead again, this time there was no accompaniment. We rode another hour south until the trees thickened and the vegetation was plush.

"This looks good." Kat added, pulling up the reins and halting her horse.

We pulled over the horses over and made camp a few hours short of freedom. We just needed to last the night.

Chapter 17

The rising sun awakened us. Stealing fruit and vegetables had become easy as we searched for wagons of locals riding to the border. A lot of people were heading North in search of work, I assumed as we trotted towards the border. We were close. Hats worn tipped down, hiding our faces, we snuck in a caravan again of Mexican families riding near the border. A man tipped his sombrero to me. I tipped mine back. Josiah didn't, and the girls pulled theirs down further, covering their faces.

"Heading to the border?" he asked me, his eyes monitoring Josiah.

"Yeah, we're gonna head down Mexico way. Life ain't fair for lots of Americans. We're headed down to get married and live free." I'm not sure why I opened up to him, perhaps simply because he looked and sounded sincere.

"Pretty senoritas," he said. "I'd love to see their smile."

I no longer trusted the man and knew we required assistance crossing the border. "Kat, Mil, tip your cap to this man, who is helping us. Give him your best smile."

Both girls stopped their horses in order to lift their caps, exposing the sun bronzed skin and puffy dark hair that didn't drop. The girls flashed their best smiles, openly embarrassed.

"Freedom awaits you." I heard a voice and wondered if the others heard it too.

We rode to the top of a hill, wondering through the fuzzy terrain occupied with sagebrush, short stubby mesquite trees, rattlesnakes, and coyotes.

The meandering river was narrower than I imagined. The man lifted his hand, halting the entourage. His family spun around, starting their ride back. Millie bent to kiss the dusty soil. Kat followed her, and Josiah and I embraced the women.

"This might be our last day in America. Do you want to cross now?" I asked the group.

Both girls mounted the horse and proceeded down the remaining bluff to the river. We followed them. The horses lapped up some water, dropping their head in the border crossing to remove more liquid from the stream. I filled the canteens before we crossed. The water remained shallow, so that all the horses had to do was trot across.

I pulled up on the riverbank and drew to a halt. I wanted to celebrate our freedom with my girl, cousin, and Millie. We made 600 miles, mostly on horseback, some by sea, and all four of us were still breathing. We made it.

On the riverbank, we sat taking in the freedom. It didn't feel different to me. Kat disrobed, dropping her clothing on the bank, and stepped into the river. Millie followed her so that they tossed the river water on each other's body, cleansing it of generations of slavery. Josiah joined Millie in her bathing, at the same time admiring Kat's body. I laid back and relaxed, enjoying the scenery.

It reminded me of the days when the journey was a mere fruition. A smile tugged at the corner of my lips as I thought of the times I got caught watching Kat bathe in a horse-tub, with her smiling back at me as I attempted not to spy on her. Now I leaned back, smiling as she washed herself in the river, feeling accomplished. This wasn't where we'd live. My father told me stories about former slaves who escaped down here. I needed to know where they lived and how they got there. I was tired of running.

After bathing and rounding up food, we ventured out on a trail. Confident we were safe; we rode with less caution than we did North of the border, our guard up. We knew full well that if we crossed the border with ease, slave catchers also could, and rumors ran amuck in Northern Mexico. Riding up the bluffs, we followed a trail that led through a cleared path. I brought my horse to a gallop and the others soon followed. We soon hit a village that had a few markets and houses scattered about. It would become our first stop. I asked about residency and once granted; we made our way deeper into the country.

Monterrey was our destination. From there we could catch a train. Tampico was our ultimate resting place, where freed slaves from the Caribbean and other runaways settled into Mexico. It was a coastal town off the Gulf. If we trusted the abandoned ship, it was a place we might have made landfall. At least we could scrape up work in Monterrey, doing odd jobs to pay for train tickets with horse compartments.

They warned us that catchers roamed the area, causing banditos up in this area to be quite handy with a pistol and often freed the slaves. Catchers had no legal right in Mexico for the capture. They were free game.

I learnt it would take three days to get to Monterrey by horse. We had all three horses. Josiah rode with Millie behind, while Kat and I rode up front beside each other. We took our time in the Mexico sun to give the horses well deserved breaks. The trail was free of catchers, which was a good sign as we rode peacefully to Monterrey. Freedom had privileges.

We sold Clete's horse and made extra money for train tickets.

"Stop right there," a voice barked in broken English. We were in the market searching for the best price.

Kat and I froze. Josiah and Millie continued riding, ignoring the pistolero.

"Me Llamo Esteban Fuertes. You cannot go any further."

Josiah still ignored the man.

"I own this land. You may not pass." The man turned his focus on my cousin and his gal, ignoring Kat and me.

Millie attempted to speak but her singing voice echoed Mexico's countryside.

"Swing low, sweet chariot

Commin' for to carry me home

Swing low, sweet chariot

Commin' for to carry me home

Well now they're commin for to carry me home"

She sounded ready for death. Senor Fuentes flipped the lasso; the rope circled Millie, and she flopped on the ground bottom first. Senor Fuentes ran to her, pulling her up.

Josiah pointed his pistol at Senor Fuentes, and with no warning fired his weapon. The Hispanic man lay dead with blood seeping through his shirt. Millie ran to Josiah, no longer crooning the spiritual. Snipers taking cover behind the rail car shot at Millie. She fell slowly as she approached her man, the song about the chariot taking her home remained in the sky. I fumbled for my pistol, but arms grabbed us, and pistols pointed at our heads. We froze and remained silent.

Josiah bent over his gal. I saw tears drip from his eyes. He looked at me and Kat, his eyes full of questions, wondering what the devil was happening. His glance went from his deceased girlfriend to his captured cousin and girlfriend, and to the train tracks where the gunshots came from. He buried his face into Mil's body again before rising with a face of death. In this state, he didn't care about Kat's and my survival, or his own.

"They set me up," he screamed, pointing a pistol at Kat and me. "They did not shoot the two of them. They set me up."

The gun remained aimed at us. Gunfire rang out, drowning the noise from streets. Men taking siestas outside the saloons woke up. Josiah tumbled to the dust in a crimson stained shirt. Kat and I attempted to run to him and right away we were met with pistols.

"You're coming with us."

Kat's and my hands received a wrapped rope behind our back and the militia yanked the rope tight. Sure we were not running any time soon, they prodded us behind our back with the butt of their guns. In this way, we marched towards a prison. Police tossed Josiah and Mil's corpses into a cart. That was the last I saw of them as they rolled out of town.

I finally spoke after a long silence. "Why? Why were they murdered, and where are we going?"

A translator relayed their message to Kat and me. "He killed Senor Fuentes, a leader of the state. Fuentes owns most of this land and that boy shot him."

I spoke to the translator. "The man attacked his girlfriend."

"The girl wanted to die, thus he did too."

Kat stood still, her faced lacked any emotion.

She blurted out to the man, "Why were we spared?"

"There's a reason you two are to be spared." His tone was stoic, ghostlike, with no emotion.

I peeked at Kat. She might have known and was not telling. The man led us to the train station. I signed papers for the two bodies that the railroad was sending onto

Louisiana. Kat and I boarded a train for Tampico. I didn't realize I signed up for the Mexican army. My Quaker upbringing opposed war, but I'd fight for my beliefs, and for those who gave me my sense of conscious. God, my father and Kat.

Part II

Chapter 18

Freed slaves settled in the coastal town of Tampico, on the eastern side of Mexico near the border. It was also a city I scouted if we sailed. Instead, two of us rode steel wheels across the Mexican countryside from Monterey to the coastal town.

The wheels clanged on the tracks as the engine picked up speed, reminding me of the harmonica riffs that Kat's father played in their shanty. A tear ran down Kat's cheek, while her foot tapped to the sound of the train accelerating.

"Reminds you of something?" I asked her.

She raised her eyes, not sure of what I meant. She brushed the tears away with both hands. "No, Robert. Millie and Josiah didn't have to die. We didn't need the juju."

"Juju?" I sat on the floor of the railcar; not sure I understood her.

"That man in Beaumont and Millie's family both came from Haiti. That big boat we took was a Haitian boat with escaped slaves who died for us and all who escaped."

She continued, sensing my ignorance of African juju customs. "That man in Beaumont is still living for a reason, and that's because of the dead people on the ship. The dead bodies got us here, that and your bravery."

I stared at her, saddened by the loss of my cousin and having had to watch his and Mil's body loaded on a different train and returned to Louisiana for Uncle Zeke to claim.

"Did you that notice Josiah acted different since he looked at the corpses? Could they have taken his soul at that time?"

Kat's knotty hair flipped in the breeze of the open rail car as she pondered the possibility. "I know it doesn't work that way."

"Could it be possible?"

"With juju, anything is possible."

They are both heroes then. Sacrificing their lives for us."

Her lips up curled, showing off her teeth. "You got it, my future husband."

"I don't understand any of this. Do we need to pay this God off, or will I have to change my beliefs?"

"It's something my family did not practice, since we wanted favors from your uncle. What I know is Josiah and Millie paid with their lives. As far as I know, the Gods received their payment."

The train continued to chug west, leaving me to think about Kat's and my future. I kept my head down, watching her fall asleep with her head in my lap as we continued our journey into freedom.

The train's speed began to fall back. For some reason, I expected a hero's welcome, with the townspeople welcoming us with a parade, dropping confetti on us as soon as we brushed the Mexican soil. I did something amazing, even though two didn't finish the journey. Kat and I were free to get married, raise a family, and begin our life together. I followed Kat down the stairs of the railcar, so that together we took in the tropical air. The smell of the sea rushed us as we scanned the town, which was about to be home.

Buildings appeared stacked on each other. Civilians scuttled about town like the ants that often ruined Josiah's and Mil's afternoon rendezvouses. To the east, I could make out the port that harbored small ships in the bay, larger than the one I tried to sail around Houston before it began sucking in water. I wondered if Kat or Millie's family were once cargo destined here.

The train kept chugging toward the coast. Tampico wasn't that far. Kat and I were anxious to join our new community and live in freedom as man and wife. Upon arrival in the coastal village, we were met by other runaways, who escorted us into the city. It was by far the largest city I've ever been in.

Blacks, Mexicans, and whites blended with small signs of prejudice, but nothing like we were used to. Children from two to eleven wandered the dusty streets, chasing dogs. Blacks, whites, Hispanics and indigenous, with all kinds of mixes involved. The community seemed friendly, and we were ready to settle in.

Kat spotted a mulatto child. "I bet our kids will look like him."

I cringed at being a parent in societies where I'll be raising a minority. I already knew before leaving Louisiana that this was a possibility, but never accepted the reality.

We stayed in a shack on the wharf, where the indigenous and immigrants worked the bay, taking the skiffs into the Gulf and taking our haul into the market. Kat stayed behind to aid the women in weaving, cooking and tending to the wandering children.

Time slipped by as we started our lives as Mexican citizens. In exchange for our freedom, I already enlisted in the Mexican army. War loomed with France, and I had to defend my new country. Quakers opposed war and promoted peace. I wasn't ready for this, and Kat wasn't ready to be abandoned, but I had no choice. Our freedom depended on it.

Father and I exchanged letters once we settled in our Tampico hut. He kept me abreast of the pending wars. The one in my current country Mexico and the one developing north of me, the war between the Union Army and the Confederacy. Before we fled, I told Josiah that if any Yank came shooting up, I'd fight for my state. Even a pacifist Quaker had his limit. I'd fight for Kat and the measly acre and cabin Pa inherited from his father. His brother Zeke got the plantation. Abolitionists received treatment higher than slaves and other minorities in Louisiana or the other end of my family. My father held onto different beliefs and was not afraid to show them. The freedom trails of the underground railroad were unknown to almost everyone but me and my cousins.

Serving Mexico was payment for the freedom Kat and I now had. Looking back, having ran away to seek freedom seemed to be a coward's way, but my people, the landowners, the party of my uncle, the establishment which surrounded me were also our oppressors. The Puritans and pilgrims fled oppression and time rewarded them. I wondered if school marms would teach our heroic flees from the tyranny of the institution. Would my father, a player in the aid of heroic flees, be mentioned? Though for obvious reasons, he would prefer his anonymity.

If ever anyone wrote my story and the rest of the freed people who settled in the coastal towns of Mexico down, some of us would prefer to be unknown. There were men who craved recognition for their duties. They made it hard for people like my late cousin and I, since I wasn't trying to change the world. All I wanted was to live my life with the woman I loved and raise a family. I couldn't do that in Louisiana or anywhere else in the country to the North. Marriage between the races was taboo and illegal.

Pa told me that Mexico abolished slavery around 1830. The people brought over were destined for the United States or the Caribbean. I bet that explained the hijacked ships scattered throughout the harbor. I needed work and figured the harbor was the best option. I managed a job loading silver into the port, which was a chief export. Other suspicious imports and exports happened as well. Being new to the country and a minority, I thought it best to keep my mouth shut. Trafficking was still rampant, even though Mexico outlawed slavery and capturing runaways.

The other men working in the shipyard were all freed slaves. We worked together, which even as an abolitionist, it still seemed awkward sharing the workload. Though it was what I believed, it wasn't what I was accustomed to. White men ruled the roost from my experience. Working hand in hand with black men took practice and some getting used to. I wasn't the boss. In fact, my boss was an immigrant from Western Africa. He worked harder than Zeke's crew and was the hardest working man I knew. He bossed the way I respected. Led by example. If I remained working for my uncle, I'd use the same technique. Field workers and hired hands respected a boss who ain't afraid to get dirty.

Kat and I lived in a housing district near the bay. The unit might have had one hundred square feet, small, no plumbing, but after being on the run for months, it was home, and we enjoyed our freedom.

Other escapees made up the other homes in the industrial housing complex. They set it up for workers in the harbor, who had made the perilous journey across Texas or across the Gulf. No one cared about cramped conditions. Freedom enchanted both us and we did not care if the Mexican government was exploiting the freedmen.

The residents were busy getting settled and providing for their families. That didn't squelch the conversations between the former runaways and freedom seekers, as well transient indigenous people.

Soon, echoes of upcoming wars shot throughout the large-converted home and the shipyard. A War Between the States up north and one happening in my new home country between Mexico and France. I didn't want to fight in either of them. Instead, I walked across the yard from our small home and worked every day to return at the end of a twelve-hour shift to a delicious dinner prepared by my bride, enjoying her charms I noticed from across the cotton fields months ago. Now I enjoyed her body and soul in private and we made love in the proper fashion. She was worth the wait.

Kat and I discussed children and raising a family, yet nothing happened. We got married about two months after arrival in Tampico. Children, however, did not come even though we asked God for a beautiful baby. We might have asked the wrong God. Six months into our stay, I received a letter from my father.

Mexico was a land of turmoil, much like the country to the North of them. In 1861, war broke out north of us. State's rights and slavery were the main ignitors of the skirmish. I admired the stance of my state, Louisiana. I didn't approve of some laws they passed, but as long as they opposed the Union's slaughter of innocent rebels, I was fine with them.

I followed the news of the war through telegraph messages and letters from my father.

MY SON ROBERT.

IT STILL SADDENS ME TO HEAR ABOUT JOSIAH AND MILLIE. I TRUST YOU AND KATHERINE ARE DOING WELL. BAD NEWS FROM HOME. LOUISIANA GOVERNMENT HAS VOTED TO SECEDE FROM THE UNITED STATES. I AGREE WITH CERTAIN RESOLUTIONS, BUT ALSO DISAGREE WITH THE KEY POINTS. IT LOOKS LIKE WAR WILL BE IN THE NEAR FUTURE, AND YOU KNOW I DETEST WAR.

MILES TAYLOR, THE REPRESENTATIVE FROM NEW ORLEANS, ALSO WARNED ABOUT WAR IF THE NORTHERN ARMIES BLOCKADED THE MISSISSIPPI RIVER AND THE PORTS OF LOUISIANA, INCLUDING LAKE CHARLES. I PRAY FOR YOUR SAFETY.

My father's letter and snippets of conversations between my fellow freedmen worried me.

"President Juarez needs to pay the debts."

"The French are coming back after us. They will invade to collect their money."

"War broke out between the states. We might be free up North."

"We never be free up there." The freedman who had been in Tampico the longest spoke out. His voice boomed over the others, and we all looked to him as a leader.

The men spoke while sitting on the soil, playing some cards. Most never looked up while speaking.

In between the buzz of voices echoing through the shipyard, one boss called me into the office. I met a short stocky Mestizo.

"Senor Barnum, I know you have been a hard worker and you and your esposa have been welcomed here. However, with the war up north and pending war here, you will have to make a choice. We need every available man to head to Puebla."

"I'm a Quaker, and don't believe in war."

Soft pleading eyes contorted into a cold, glassy stare. I understood it meant that his previous request wasn't a question. "Senor Barnum, then you would have no choice but to return to the United States and take your spouse with you. You will face the consequences of any legal action against you. I heard through your government that you are still a wanted man- wanted dead or alive."

I swallowed hard. It felt like gravel going down my throat. "Will fighting for this country allow us to be citizens?"

He ignored my question instead accepting my inquiry as a volunteer. "Report to the Army office down the road," he said, pointing to an uninhabited building near our residence.

I headed towards the building, but turned and gazed over the bay, drooling at the port.

Senor Fuentes hollered, "Now Barnum. You must volunteer."

I looked back at the man. In my mind, I saw a machete in hand, ready to slash the closest thing in sight. That was me. I reversed direction and made a beeline for the enlistment office.

Three men in blue uniforms with bullet vests crisscrossed over their chest soon followed me down the cobblestone walk and escorted me into a room without chairs. There, I signed my life away.

To continue our freedom, I volunteered to fight for the Mexican army. A return to the northern country would mean life on the run or death at the border. Life in Mexico was not perfect or safe, not with the constant fear of slave catchers, and we always had concern of the betrayal of our current government., as well as our allies. There was no age or religious restrictions to enrolling in the Mexican army. Being a Quaker didn't help my cause, neither being seventeen.

"Dear, I have to go. The train leaves in the morning." I brushed Kat's cheek with the back of my had, wiping off droplets of water that fell from her wide, brown eyes. "You know I don't want to go. I'm not sure why they are fighting. Seems to me the government is welching out on some debts to Europeans."

"Everything is hearsay, Robert. I'm sure we will never know the truth." She was a smart one.

"That's what the guys working the docks were saying, but we're dealing with governments, plus we got war back up north. I need to write my father a letter."

Father:

KAT AND I ARE FINE. WE HAVE LEARNED THE LANGUAGE. LIFE IS SCARY DOWN HERE. I HEARD THE FRENCH ARE ON THEIR WAY TO MEXICO TO FORCE THE PAYMENT OF A DEBT. SINCE I'M A MEMBER OF THE MILITARY, THEY HAVE REQUESTED ME TO TRAVEL TO PUEBLA ALONG WITH OTHER FREED SLAVES. KAT, ALONG WITH THE OTHER FREED WOMEN, MAY ACCOMPANY US.

YOUR SON,

PRIVATE ROBERT BARNUM,

MEXICAN ARMY.

"Robert, I don't want you to go. I need you here," Kat pleaded, but I owed it to my new country to fight the French. "You're against war, and you always said if you ever had to fight, you would flee to the west." Her big, brown eyes made my knees wobble as she spoke.

"We fought for survival. Since I met you, and we've been together, I've learned that fighting in battle can be beneficial, especially when it's for one you love. I owe this country for allowing us to be married and grow our relationship. It is my obligation."

"Stay with me. I'm alone and I need you beside me." Her arms went around my shoulders, mine wrapped around her waist.

We conversed most of the evening, besides making love and getting my rest. The conversation continued as we strolled towards the train station.

I pulled her close, our bodies pressed into each other. I murmured softly into her ear. "I love you. You're the reason I'm doing this" I kissed her neck and ears.

The train was due any minute. I didn't want it to come. Her petite body pressed against mine made me think of other things, along with her sweet fragrance.

Reading my mind, she grasped my hand and pulled me behind an abandoned adobe hut. She raised her dress and tossed it on the soil. Her dark skin was beautiful, breasts firm and stood at attention. She leaned back on her dress, looking inviting as ever. She was accepting that this would be a final escapade before battle. She looked so inviting, and the climax happened quicker than either of us wanted.

"I'll be safe in Puebla," I promised. "I will return as soon as I can."

She smiled, not satisfied by the performance, but still enjoying the bliss of its aftermath.

She cooed in my ear. "I know you will. I wanted you one more time before you left." She turned, bent over, and shook her backside at me, at the same time lifting her dress off the sunbaked Mexican clay soil. She dashed towards me and planted a kiss on my lips as the train's volume increased.

"I love you, Robert." She pulled me close.

"I love you too, Kat." I kissed her forehead and then the cheek.

As she walked towards the village, the smoke from the steam engine became visible in the western sky. Tears descended fast on my face as I watched her hurry away, head down but refusing to look back. I turned to the oncoming train and waited until it slowed to a stop.

I entered with the other soldiers. Mostly slaves mixed in with Mexican men and a couple of white men, possibly with similar stories as mine.

The train headed down the gulf coast to the town of Veracruz. It was an eight- hour train ride along the edge of the Bay of Campeche. To take my mind off the ache in my heart, I admired the vegetation and the jungle that soon controlled the scenery. With the new development, the letters to my father diminished. Instead, my communication with my wife took priority, as well as my survival.

Chapter 19

Pueblo, Mexico
May 1862.

Puebla was key to Mexico's success. Between the port of Vera Cruz and the capital, Mexico City, a downtrodden group of freed blacks and Mexicans and I boarded the rail to save the city.

One of the Generales spoke to us in Spanish. By this time, I held a grasp of the language. I wasn't fluent but could make words and phrases out. The commander spoke slowly, aware that there were groups from north of the border.

"Viva México. Estamos parando a los franceses en Puebla. Quieren un estado independiente en Puebla. Debemos combatirlos. ¡Viva México!"

I looked to one of the Mexicans, who spoke the best English. "They want to make a state of Puebla," he confirmed.

Even as an anti-war youth, I felt excited. I made a fist and raised my right arm, drawing applause from the crowd.

Most of the Mexicans cheered, ready to battle and fight for their war-torn country. I sat beside a freedman from the Beaumont area, only to discover that he knew Sock, the man we met and who led us to freedom, or in Josiah and Millie's case, their death.

"Da man is a quack. Ain't no spirits on those boats." He looked at me with mistrust.

I had dealt with Kat's family and the other slaves. I was the same as Uncle Zeke in his eyes.

"Why you here?" His eyes brightened.

"I stole a woman, and we got married in Tampico. She was my uncle's property" I kept a copy of a waybill poster ripped off a storefront window with my picture. I reached into my bag and showed it to him. He struggled with reading. "It says, WANTED DEAD OR ALIVE. I can't go back. I always thought owning people was immoral, and in fact the government didn't see you as people but property. That's why my cousin and I stole the girls and fled here. We wanted to raise families down here."

"You two survived, your cousin and his gal died. She came over the same way I did. I like you, son." The man was twice my age. "We need to stick together, so we'll survive this."

"I don't believe in no spirits. I don't care if they got me this far." I stared straight into his eyes.

"I don't believe either. It's a battle. Strength in numbers, boy."

"How did you escape?"

He looked at me, afraid to reveal his secret. "I strangled the overseer, stole his gun. Then I shot the owner in Beaumont. Been here for three years now."

I looked away at this hardened man who killed for freedom. I wondered if he took other lives on the lam or killed if survival depended on it. I remained silent the rest of the way and penned letters to Kat and my father in my head. When we arrived in the city, I intended to write them down. I kept my head down and prayed a quick Quaker prayer for a rapid end to the coming battle.

The train arrived in Puebla on the evening of May 3, 1862.

The letters I wrote to Kat and my father were similar, however the personalization ended different.

DEAREST KAT.

I LOVE YOU. YOU MAKE MY WORLD. ONCE THIS BATTLE WAS OVER, I WAS TOLD I COULD RETURN. I MISS YOU AND OUR LOVEMAKING. WE WILL GROW A FAMILY ONCE THE BATTLE IS OVER. I WANT SEVERAL KIDS AND A BIG FARM IN LOUISIANA. ONCE THE WAR UP NORTH IS OVER, WE CAN LIVE FREE AS MAN AND WIFE. UNTIL THEN, WE WILL STAY IN MEXICO. I'M LEARNING TO LOVE THE PEOPLE I AM DEPLOYED WITH.

AS SOON AS POSSIBLE, I WANT TO RETURN. I ALREADY MISS YOUR TOUCH. I NEVER THOUGHT IT WOULD FEEL AS GOOD AS IT DOES. YOU ARE A SPECIAL WOMAN, AND WE WOULD NOT HAVE MADE IT IF IT WASN'T FOR YOUR DECISIONS. I THINK OF JOSIAH AND MILLIE EVERY DAY AND WONDER WHAT PLAY THE SPIRITS HAD IN MAKING OUR DESTINATION. ON THE TRAIN DOWN, I MET A MAN FROM BEAUMONT, A NON-BELIEVER. HE CALLED THE MAN WHO AIDED US A SELL-OUT.

THE TROOPS ARE READY. I HOPE TO RETURN BY THE TIME YOU RECEIVE THIS LETTER.

LOVE, ROBERT.

The letter to my father was similar about war. I asked him to pray for me, excluding the talks of passion between my bride and me. I hadn't heard from my father. The last letter discussed war breaking out. Letters take time to cross countries, however I worried about his safety.

Unknown to me, and also Kat, the Mexican Army also wanted the women to join. Male soldiers required support women that would take care of them. At first, when we heard about an outbreak of war, Kat and I would often argue about the gender roles.

"Robert, you know us women can fight in battle. It ain't about skill or strength, but how much hate you have in your heart, and I got lots of hate in here. I'd think those French people are Mastah Zeke and the rest of the staff. I got no problem killing them. There is a lot of pain right here." She struck her chest, right below her breasts. "Robert, so you need to be careful the way you talk to me and treat me. I can do anything and will."

I had skills required for battle, mainly the roping and riding. My heart didn't believe in killing, and why should I kill for a battle between two powerful men who sought to invade each other? Most wars were about money or independence, while this potential battle in Mexico was about both.

Kat never received the letter. She and the other women who joined the army boarded a train the following day to the fort city.

She found me at the fort and hurried towards me with arms open for a big hug. I met her with a glare. "What in the devil are you doing here?" I asked.

Kat bowed her head. All excitement vanished from her face. A grimace replaced her beautiful smile, and a tear formed.

"Robert, the women are here to support you. We'll cook and do the special things you like when there is privacy. We can fight if needed. A lot of women down here can kill a Frenchman as good as you men."

175

I still didn't want her there, though I was glad she was with me. It was the 1860's. Women fought in previous American wars; but my views remained that woman stay home. It didn't matter what type of soldier they would make; my wife would be the best and with some luck even lead a platoon.

They stationed Kat and me at Fort Guadalupe. Fort Loreto protected the city of Puebla, looming above the city at a high elevation. I peeked out one of the holes designated for rifles and could see the valley below. I could even make out a marching Frenchman carrying the blue, white, and red flags and muskets, and claiming Mexico as a French territory and reinstating slavery. There was a reason we revolted, and a large reason the freed aided their adopted country.

Quarters were not private. Kat's duties began as a cook, preparing meals for the troops. She learnt to cook from her mother back on Zeke's plantation. This was the role I accepted for my bride. I didn't want either of us in combat. Yet, it seemed that the rage of being a slave since birth, except for the last year, still carried inside Kat like a baby emerging, she wanted a more combative role. General Porfirio Diaz agreed to this request after a dinner she prepared on May 3. They chose her to go with a team of Mexicans to work as guerilla fighter out of the neighboring fort, Fort Loreto. I was assigned to follow, since my work was best done on horseback with a whip, lasso, and a bow and arrow.

Soladeras prepared the morning meal on May 5th. It was an early morning. Women prepared tortillas and beans, a standard breakfast for us Mexicans. Most troops scarfed their food without a thought in a rush to get ready for battle. I took dainty bites, salvaging my meal in case it was my last.

The leading General had total faith in his and President Juarez's strategy. He spoke to us at the fort. We stood tall in our boots, our worn-out uniforms well pressed.

"You are fighting the best and most discipline armies in the world." He strode around the soldiers. "But you are the first sons of Mexico."

We cheered, including newly adopted citizens as myself and other freedmen, former slaves and abolitionists who joined the battle.

"Viva Mexico!" we chanted in loud screams, all ready for war.

Spinning around in my station, I turned to peer down the valley. Our troops had a perfect view downslope. I spotted them. Our scouts predicted that these men would arrive today. Through the field glasses, I noticed the men's confident stride, like this would be no battle. The war would be like trouncing ants marching in a spare room. Flags wave, arrogant French smiles plastered on their faces, they stopped and set up camp as the cannons stopped. We were in striking distance and hollered across the fort to stand guard.

A deafening explosion echoed through the quarters. Craters with bodies swallowed inside grew in numbers. Kat in the other quarters was in the middle of being trained in guerilla warfare. Right now, my job was to shoot and protect my adopted country, but I fled to protect my wife. I snuck across the hilltop to the adjacent building. The horses remained at Loreta, while the brutal first took out many Mexican and freed slaves. I was ready to go on offense.

"Senor Barnum," a larger man, stoic in stature, wore spectacles and above average height and weight, called to me.

I didn't know many people, but word got around that I was a horseman and good with a whip.

"We need you with the guerillas." General Zaragosa spoke.

I recognized the markings on his blue uniform. "Yes, sir."

I turned to salute the leader.

"We need you to aid the Indigenous in the fields. You sprinted by them, and I admired your speed and handling of el caballo."

"In all due respect, sir, I saw no one in the fields."

"Exactly," the leader spoke. "They remain hidden. I have a whip and machete ready for you. Hide with the Indigenous."

I turned but still spotted no one. A smile formed on my face. I was ready for guerilla warfare.

I felt for my Louisiana brothers up north, the men and boys who fought to protect their land. This is what we were doing south of the border, protecting the nation from The French invading our land. Up north wasn't all about slavery. My father and I opposed and did what we could. We didn't own slaves but had property which we loved, including small amounts of livestock and grew our own fruits and vegetables. There were more like us in Dixie.

The mud that enveloped my body kept me in camouflage. I changed out of my army uniform into a sleeker native attire. With my whip, machete, bows and arrows, I crept back into the foliage. Another officer pointed me towards the guerillas, where we will wait until called upon to attack.

I sat under a forest of date trees along with other vegetation. I recognized a fellow guerilla fighter a few feet away. The vegetation was thick, but I made out the French troops marching up. Their strides were long as they carried their weapons in their red uniforms. Their eyes were bright and wide.

Most of my troop carried only machetes. I raised the field glasses again with attention to the speed of the advancing soldiers. They marched in unison, getting closer as they marched up the hill.

The group waited for orders from General Diaz who watched nearby. Mexico was not France and through the whispers of the freedmen, France wanted to enforce slavery. Maybe it was a method of firing the Americans up more, or there might have been truth to the rumors. I wasn't sure. All I knew was that I needed to fend for Mexico and do whatever it took.

The hush in the forest was deafening. We tucked away in silence, keeping a watchful eye on the protruding foreigners. Their speed decreased as they climbed. It would only be minutes before we wagered a counterattack. An attack which Generals Diaz and Zaragosa would leave the French sprawled in pools of their own blood.

We waited for the call. Our troops were ready when it eventually came. Natives I hadn't seen attacked the French with machetes, slashing with the blade. I watched a lone soldier keep climbing the hill, from where he fired into the bushes and reloaded the musket. He was twenty feet from me and kept marching, firing and reloading.

He aimed away from me and got into a clearing. The Frenchman's focus was in the shrubbery in the opposite direction. He fired into the trees, hoping to nail a victim. I seized the opportunity when he stopped to reload. I flicked the rope and nailed him, sending his rifle and him to the ground. I sprinted towards him, machete in the air, screaming like a rebel, and whipped the blade across his throat. I dashed into the bushes and rekindled the rope. This time they searched my direction, but guerillas came from the other side attacking. Three more French lay dead at the top of the ridge. Lord knows how many never climbed the bluff.

Another invader made his way towards me. He appeared confident that the march to capture the city would be easy, even after observing the slaughter of his comrades. His focus was on my hiding spot, while my rope was ready to go. I flung it through the clearing, whipping the rifle from his hands. Then I dashed towards the stunned soldier, machete waving. He never stood a chance. Blood and veins stained my machete blade. I wiped it off on a palm leaf and crawled back in with my blood-stained machete.

The French leader made a call as the surviving French returned down the slope in retreat. The clouds in the sky burst as a rainstorm descended on Puebla. The natives were well versed in the terrain, but I was a swamp rat, used to mud of the bayou, as our contingent chased foreign invaders down the hill, taking out as many as we could kill.

The French got on horseback. I joined in with the Calvary on horseback and rode side by side with General Diaz to give chase until Zaragosa called us off. We didn't have enough ammunition left to finish the butchering. General Diaz led us back, with me wanting to take the lead.

We rode back to the fort victorious. I was unaware of the significance of the battle. I never knew the French had never lost a battle since 1812 and that The Mexican Army never fought off a foreign intruder. I stood in the forefront, a hero to the Mexican people and President Benito Juarez himself.

We stayed in Fort Guadalupe, working hard to round up the lifeless bodies from the original cannon shots, as well as access the damage on our side. Kat helped make dinner and gave me a hero's welcome later that evening.

Chapter 20

Days after the battle, the Mexican army still had a need for me. I remained in the brush and raided transports and supply depots, as well as killed roaming Frenchman. We resided in Puebla for a few months. Returning to Tampico was not an option. My country needed me, and Kat and I needed a home.

We easily defeated the French in the first battle, but knew they'd return stronger than ever with more troops, a better arsenal, and new leadership. Being a guerrilla fighter, I did what I could to make the French stay in Mexico a living hell, while they waited for reinforcements.

Kat and I spent little time together. Soldaderas were busy working at other forts or moved to Mexico City. Kat had settled in the capital city, leaving me alone with the fellow guerrillas. We waited on reinforcements and used the wait to obliterate anything resembling French possessions including stranded soldiers.

I carried dynamite with me riding through the hills to Orizaba, where the remaining French soldiers hid. Anything that looked like it belonged to France, I lit a wand of TNT from atop my horseback and tossed it into the depot to sabotage buildings, supplies or soldiers.

Since I was better and quicker with a rope than a gun, I took pleasure with hostages. I carried my machete in case the lassoed prisoner got too feisty. My pacifist ways vanished to the reality of war as my cold-blooded killing sped up.

Six months went by. Guerilla fighters and I roamed the countryside impairing anything French. I finally got a leave and proceeded to Mexico City to visit my bride. November 1862 found Kat and thousands of others set up sanctuary in the capital city. Kat had stayed there the last month, while I butchered the countryside between Puebla and Orizaba.

Kat prepared beans and tortillas for the male soldiers. I watched her with a smile. Her appearance displayed no emotion. After traveling with her, I knew what that meant, an argument waited in the future. It wasn't something I ever saw myself doing, but war changed people. It changed me.

She plopped beans on a soldier's plate and threw him a tortilla. He exited the line of tired troops to flop on the soil and refresh his soul. The line extended several soldiers deep, causing Kat to continue the mistreatment of the hungry warriors. She continued plopping and tossing the beans and corn tortillas at the men. Kat was creating a ration system in her service.

She saw me watching and dropped her utensils, not minding that the morose and tedious line of troops lingered. I noticed the faces of the desperate starving men, some whom I served with, watch her sprint towards me. Squints and scowls flashed on the men, who closed their fists in frustration. Two more freed slaves followed Kat in abandoning the starving men.

She grabbed my hand and led me from the messy hall and towards the barracks across the fort's interior. I wanted to mention her disobedience to her duty, but one look at the rage on her face made me think twice.

We sat alone in a make-shift barrack after discovering a vacant room in Castillo de Chapultepec, the largest fort in the capital. Her small but firm breasts nuzzled against my chest. I caressed her bottom, at the same time enjoying twirling her hair around my finger.

"Robert, you are a lucky man to be placed right in the middle of the action. You're fighting for your freedom. I admire you for thoughts and word from the generals to the people. They say you are a hero."

"Darling, I ain't no hero. Killing folk ain't heroic."

She cut me off. "I wish I was out there fighting instead of being a servant. You took me off your uncle's plantation because I was a servant and property to the fat man. Now I'm doing the same thing. I'm cooking and serving these dirty, greasy men, along with my sisters, the other Adelitas." She took a deep breath. "I want to fight with the men."

I had to man up and tell her how I felt. She had no business in war. Women did not fight in battle. A man's job was to protect, especially his wife.

I put my feet down, drawing a proverbial line in the sand. "I don't want you to. War is a man's game, darling. I don't want to fight, but I'm fighting for the freedom of Mexico, our adopted country. So, I'm fighting for you and all freed slaves here, as well as the people who took us in."

She pushed herself up and stood naked above me. No smile appeared as her lips. Her eyes were glassy, and not bright. "You don't understand, but I'm not a servant, honey. Do you realize I've been a slave all my life until I was a fugitive? I was nothing more than a piece of property and now I'm glorified property. There is so much fire in me caused by your uncle, and do you know what? The French would bring back slavery. I need to fight and kill every Frenchman who comes onto the soil. I've proved to be a better shot than you. I helped us escape and survive. You and me wouldn't have made it without either of us."

"Darling, I want you safe so we can build a life together. We could do that here, or when it's safe to go back home we could return to Louisiana. I love you and care about your well-being." I knew from the look on her face that my arguments would fall on deaf ears.

"Why did you drag me into this war infested nation then? Why didn't we go north with the established railroad?"

I admired her intelligence but loathed the questions. "This was quicker to get out of the country. Just because you get out of the South doesn't mean you're free. Some of Uncle Zeke's slaves we left behind made it as far as Northern Ohio when they got caught. Slave catchers are everywhere."

"I'm sorry, Robert," Kat said without emotion. She turned her head, not looking at me, and found her clothing. "I talked to General Zaragosa before he got ill, when we were still in Puebla." She stepped away, almost afraid to tell me.

"What's wrong?"

"Robert, they want me to ride between here and Puebla and down to Orizaba and become a messenger. I have a right to shoot any French I see."

"You know I'm not the bossy type, but I only want you safe. I won't forbid you to go, but I have said my piece. I want you behind these walls." I pointed towards the exterior of the shelter.

"You've made General Diaz, Ortega and even Zaragosa recognize you. President Juarez even knows your name, but Robert, I'm meaner than you. I'm sure killing Frenchmen came difficult for you. It won't for me. I see your uncle and his drunk overseer in every Frenchmen, and I have a license to kill."

"Trust me darling, you don't want to kill, not even the enemy. I've killed and it's contagious. Thank God I'm on leave, though still agitated. I need to return to the brush, since all I want to do is kill a French person. The new commander sensed it and gave me a pass. That's the only reason I'm here right now.

An officer barged in and noticed both our naked bodies. He spoke in Spanish. "Excuse me, I need to speak with the lady in private. Cover yourself and we can find another room to talk."

Kat tossed her uniform on and staggered towards the officer, returning a few minutes later.

She returned to where I was stretched out on the mud floor of a vacant room in the fort and squatted next to me. "They have assigned me to ride with you back to Puebla. Once there, I'm to ride to where the French camp out and gather as much information as I can regarding the return of their soldiers."

"Do I ride with you?"

"No, they know most of the guerrillas. The French are unaware of soldaderas, especially Negroes."

"So, we leave together?"

"Yes. General Ortega granted it. When your pass is over, we return to Fort Guadalupe and wait for assignments."

"I don't like this one bit, but I'm not forbidding you. At least we can be together." I shook my head. I needed her to be safe, as well as try to understand her rage.

I threw my clothes on in a rush to join the other soldiers and soldaderas for an afternoon meal. A meal Kat should have helped prepare.

Two days passed and the two of us left Mexico City for Puebla, now named Puebla de Zaragoza after the late general, who succumbed to typhoid months earlier. It was a three-day ride through the mountainous terrain. I liked to test my horse and Kat kept up her steed galloping beside mine.

We built small fires to keep the predators away and for warmth, then went hunting and gathering additional food. We packed our bags with meals we could carry, including nuts and fruit. Nailing an antelope with an arrow wasn't out of the question. Kat nailed one on the first day out and stripped it clean for us to cook on the fire.

I did not doubt her survival skills. She had made it this far working with her family on a plantation and then on the run with Josiah, Millie and me. She got us out of several disasters, and we wouldn't have made it to Mexico if it wasn't for her and her trusted leadership. But I just wanted her safe. We were in a war-torn country, as was the country to our north, fighting amongst themselves.

We enjoyed private time with the campfire keeping coyotes and wolves away, and in two days rode into Fort Guadalupe to await assignments. I was out of action for a week and missed the destruction and blood.

We were in luck to ride together to Orizaba the day after we arrived at the fort. With mountains exceeding 16,000 feet, the ride wouldn't be easy, however the terrain was one reason we won the initial battles. That and the heart of the guerrillas. We'd ride together, husband and wife, through the mountainous terrain, up and down the slopes, searching for a stranded Frenchman to knock off or any replaced arsenal to send into the sky. The ride began in vain, as we spotted nothing out of the ordinary.

I knew the area well during my time riding, hiking and destroying the scenery with sticks of dynamite if it was a potential French supply depot. On this trip, they had replaced no depots in the area. Maybe another fighter would spot one off route, or the enemy might wait for reinforcements. Kat's job was to find out when additional French would arrive from Europe.

We set camp up near the falls. Thunderous burbles rang out to the east of us.

"What's that roaring sound?" she asked, staring off in the direction from which the noise had come.

"From the waterfall around the corner."

We strolled close to the falls, hand in hand, exploring the soaring mountains, the green vegetation and as we turned the corner, the falls from the Rio Blanco.

"My goodness, darling." Kat stared in amazement. "They are fascinating."

"I've made this my secret spot, especially after making a kill or blowing up a depot. There are many places to disappear and believe me, I've thought about it."

She led me to the pond in which the water cascaded into. We sat under the falls enjoying the water dripping on us.

"Robert, this life is hell."

"It's got to be better than the life you led." The water continued cascading.

"I'm going crazy too. You know I see the old overseer and your uncle wearing the green and red hideous uniforms. I want to kill them with a machete, slashing over and over."

"We should desert."

She glanced at me, the water still splashing on her hat. "Where would we go? We'll be wanted in two countries."

"Kat darling." I took her face in my hand, so our eyes met. "Before all this, I never killed a person in my life. Now I'm searching for a lone stranded enemy out wandering, so I can murder him in cold blood. If I don't see anyone, and return to the fort, I'll be disappointed. It's like I must kill someone or I'm a failure."

"Robert, you'll never be a failure. You stole me off your uncle's land and made me a free woman and your wife. The Mexican army recognized you as a hero. We both need to do our jobs, and with any luck, we'll defeat the French when they return."

I sighed. "I hate war. Let's get back to camp."

We shook our heads, swishing water from our head and walked with damp bodies back to camp to feed the horses and make a small fire for dinner and protection. One of us would be on sentry, while the other would rest.

The night was uneventful. We ate some fresh fruit and washed under the falls before riding to the city. I knew exactly where they resided. My job was to lead Kat to The French fortress and retreat into the brush. We'd meet at the falls and ride back together.

After kissing her cheek for luck, I pointed out the best place to gather information. I rode back to the falls and camped where we stayed the previous night. I glanced at the doused fire. It seemed different, like the ashes were recent, not from the morning, but from earlier that evening. Someone was near. I heard and saw nothing, just an eerie silence. The enemy had been hiding out here for over six months and knew the land as well as me. My machete, whip, and rifle were ready. Riding to where the fire burnt down, I scoped the soil for clues, footprints or horse tracks to determine how many might be near. I noticed two sets of prints in the ash. They outnumbered me, but I have been outmanned in the past, yet I was clueless about their location. Surrendering now was not an option. I glanced at the tall trees near the falls and noticed a rope. French had habits of hanging us guerrilla fighters who got themselves captured.

I was a sitting duck but could outrun them on my horse. Besides, Kat would return by high noon the next day. There was no way I could leave my mate for the blood-thirsty and revenge seeking French. This was a time where I wished my steed wasn't with, since hiding a horse can be challenging. I knew the land and brush and could easily set a trap.

I tied the horse to a tree across the path from the falls and armed myself with a machete, lasso, and rifle before crawling through the brush, hoping to see them before they spotted me. The sun had begun setting, darkness crept in, yet I couldn't light a fire in fear of being taken hostage or decapitated. Kat should be back.

Darkness enveloped the valley I stayed in. Not wanting to close my eyes in fear of capture, I rested and sometime within my stay I dozed with the sun coming in over the Bay of Campeche. I snacked on fruits and jerky, then snuck around into the area of the falls, again scouting for Frenchmen.

A sound jolted me. It wasn't loud but came from an area which should have been silent. I saw nothing, then heard two male voices speaking in French. As soon as I felt a knife at my throat, I let my weapons fall into the mud. They tied my hands behind my head, but that didn't seem enough because they struck my temple with my rifle, the brute force sending me splat on the soil. My knife remained in my sheath, and I wondered how I would use it.

Hands dragged me across the ground, with no regards to the terrain. Rocks ripped the skin on my back, letting out blood that oozed out my body. They pulled me into an area with trees, high enough to make a neck split when hung properly.

The duo spoke in a quiet tone with no inflection. It was a matter-of-fact tone they conversed with as I bounced across the earth to my pending death. They hauled me to the tree. Through bruised, swollen eyes I could see one work on the noose with the rope they tugged me with. It was the rope I've had since we left Louisiana, the same rope Uncle Zeke gave to me to whip Kat's bare bottom. My hands still tied, however the knot loosened around my wrists, I struggled to free my hands. The other member of the enemy kept poking my wrists, neck and face with his knife, torturing me. I used it to my advantage to shake my hands free of their entrapment.

I looked at my two captors and wondered how to take them out. The element of surprise has worked for our side so far. My free hand reached for my small blade. Stabbing the French soldier anywhere would stun him enough to take out the noose maker, and then return to the hauler.

I clung to my knife, my eyes closed, and prayed. I prayed for salvation and prayed for the best way out of my situation. Above all, I prayed for Kat to come up riding, so she could shoot the Frenchmen down.

The man carried the rope to a tree and tossed it over a thick branch. The noose dangled low enough for my head to go through. Aware that the pair would soon hoist me, I thought stalling might be an option. At the same time, counting on French incompetence wasn't a choice.

They got the rope secured, and all they had to do was fit my head through the hole and hoist and drop me. I studied the man leading me to my death, on the lookout for a spot to stab him. I had my knife in my hand, out of the sheath.

"Robert!" the woman screamed, causing the French to divert their attention.

I bailed to the ground, and it only took two shots for Kat to drop both of them. She flailed several more into the Europeans. After the explosion of gunfire had died down, I glanced up and noticed her taking aim, making sure they became mortally wounded. I observed the frustration of being my uncle's property in her eyes, the meanness, the savagery of being owned. It was a look I never wanted to see from her. She pulled the trigger. The deceased man hopped up and splatted again on the soil. She repeated it to the other capturers I remained on the ground, while she took another round each into the two Frenchmen. I struggled to my feet unable to suppress the wince due to my scars from being dragged and poked. She dismounted and pulled me close. It was supposed to be the other way around, however I nestled into her arms. The woman gave great hugs.

I tried to recapture the ability to speak after climbing the mountains from Orizaba to Puebla. I looked at my bride, more than ever realizing I had a keeper. She saved my life and it was not the first time. "This war is killing me. One of those men was Mexican. We're fighting our own down here. We might as well return to Coushatta."

"They want you dead or alive. Once this war is over, we can be free as a couple, raise a family, be the couple you wanted when you spied on me at bath time." She rode slightly in front of me as we continued scaling the ridge.

"That was the closest to death I've faced. If it wasn't for you, I'd be swaying from a limb of a tree, and not found for weeks. I'm thinking of deserting. We both should. We've paid our dues, and Juarez has recognized both of us. Let's think about living with the indigenous up north." I kicked my horse in the gut, sending it to sprint ahead of her horse. I felt alive.

We settled on a crest on the mountain outside Orizaba. It was a full day's ride from the falls. I didn't want to stay in the valleys. It would only make us sitting ducks.

"Did you gather information?" I asked.

"Yes, I did. More men and newer equipment are on the way. I will let Ortega know once we get back."

I hung my head. "So, we'll be at war for a while?" I didn't look at her, but at the small campfire we lit.

"Robert!" she snapped, sick of my whining about the war. "We've made it this far. God is on our side."

"Which one? We've dealt with many gods so far."

"My God, the God from Africa. The man who protected us on the boat. Many slaves died, but our family didn't. The journey was a lot longer and tougher than what we've been on, and with no reward. At least we have freedom. Now, if we desert, we'll be on the run from this country and America. Robert, we must gut this out."

She was right. It was just that I missed Louisiana and my father. It had been awhile since I heard from him. I wondered about the war Between the States and how my homeland was holding up. I also wondered if the North conquered the Confederacy, could Kat and I live free as man and wife?

I didn't share my thoughts with her. We must return to Puebla and then to President Juarez to share the information. After two more days of riding, we finally arrived at Fort Guadalupe.

After Kat shared her information with an officer of the Mexican Army and some beans and tortillas, we escaped the bustling soldiers roaming the fort to seek solace and alone time. Strengthened by the trip and her saving my life, the lovemaking was the best it ever was between us. Spent and exhausted, we fell asleep afterwards.

"Corporal Robert Barnum!" the messenger shouted.

I had a letter from the United States Government. Kat was waking up. Her smile told what happened between the two of us last night. She rubbed her eyes, and lifted her bare arms over head, exposing her naked chest.

I ripped the envelope open, and the letter fell out like the French shot it from my hands.

"What is it?"

"My father." I crawled to retrieve the letter and reread it. "It says friendly fire hit and killed him. I don't believe it was a friendly fire. Someone wanted him dead. I need to find out."

"Are you going back?"

"I have to. My father had a friend in Texas who we were supposed to use. I'll head up there."

"You can't leave me here alone."

"I need to find out what happened, but personally, I think Zeke or Clete was responsible. I'll get a train ticket, sneak across the border and return once I find out what happened." A quick sigh escaped me. "I don't trust either the Confederacy or the Union, so I'll leave in the morning."

"You're gonna leave?" She turned her face away from me.

"You have plenty of support here. The soladeras love you. You've earned respect from the leadership. It will only be for a few weeks. I have to find out what happened, and I will write."

My excuses didn't help my cause. She stormed off, fist clenched, her steps erratic. I didn't see her the rest of the day. I wanted to desert the Mexican Army, and I did. I took what pay I had and took the rail to the border, where I would sneak across.

I crossed in Laredo and snuck onto a train, which led me near Jasper. It was a three-day journey. I sent my father's friend a telegraph message when the train stopped in Houston.

He met me at his house, north of town and met me at the door and let me in after searching. I was still a fugitive, a wanted man, even though it had been years since the thievery.

"Robert, how are you?" The man, now wearing a stovetop hat and groomed a thick beard, greeted me. His hair had turned gray, and he wore spectacles. He reached for me and gave me a hug. "You heard about your father; I take it?"

After catching up and telling him about life south of the border, he informed me about my father's death.

"I wasn't there. It happened at his church on your land. I can take you there. Remember Will Harris? He was there, but the Union Army let him go. However, they executed your father. Do you want to see Mr. Harris?"

"I want to hear all about it. I want to be there when it happened, and if this was an execution, I want revenge."

"We'll have to go horseback. Stages aren't running because of the war. It ain't safe."

"I figured. I don't mind riding."

We got his best horse saddled up, threw on some saddlebags, then it was time to see what happened to my father. We rode cautiously in a similar route the four of us earlier took down, through the swamps of East Texas. Gray coats scattered about, all rose with pointed rifles as we trotted past them, ready for battle. Already hardened by war fighting for the nation to the south, it numbed me.

"What happened to Josiah?" He asked as we rode side by side through a clearing that led to the Sabine.

"Mexican bandits killed him, along with Millie. I think Millie believed in them spirits and talked Josiah into sacrificing their lives for Kat and me. Some old African curse she picked up from the Caribbean."

"I never understood their religions, and that's why your uncle and his kind wanted to force the Bible on them."

"I don't either, but I've been trying to learn some of Kat's customs, too. Makes for a better world to adapt to other cultures instead of forcing yours on people enslaved."

"How is Kat?"

"Damn, I miss her already. She's great and there's no way we would have gotten out of Texas without her. Saved my life a few times, on the way down, and also in the war down there. Makes me wonder about Millie giving her life up for Kat. I really think it was true."

We camped overnight on the banks of the Sabine. My old home was across the river. We sat by the fire and continued conversing. "Where's the action at, anyway? Have seen little around here?"

"Right now, this area is quiet, too quiet. Down by Lafayette and around Vermillion Bayou, things have been heating up. Best bet is to lie low and sneak into town once we cross. We never know when the Yanks will hit. Guerrilla fighters have scattered their attacks on both sides throughout the state."

"I was a guerilla down in Mexico, sneaking up on French soldiers and shooting them in cold blood. Pa dying gave me an excuse to desert their Army."

"I hate war. I hate the enslavement we did on the colored folks almost as much as I hate war, and you know them blue bellies who come down butchering our boys don't give a damn about abolishment. The people opposed ain't fighting the battles. Most are objecting are Quaker like you, your pa and me."

"Once I find out who killed Pa, I'm enlisting. I'll take sides against who killed him."

"We'll find out tomorrow," the man said. He tugged his hat over his eyes to get a well-deserved nap.

Chapter 21

Crossing the Sabine on horseback, I noticed a young man in the distance scouting the area. He stood in the bayou, looking towards the mighty flowing river. My father's partner rode through the soft current of the Sabine inching closer, while I wondered if I rode into a trap. I prodded on, certain that my life could not end without discovering the truth.

The man inched towards us, as we approached the muddy riverbank.

"Robert Barnum," a young native man about my age called. He appeared unarmed, but out here one needed a weapon to survive, especially in the middle of a war.

It's been about four years since I wandered through this territory. I didn't recognize him at first, but then it hit me. He was the same young man who helped Josiah and me years earlier.

"You heard about your father?"

We road up towards the old home that stood with walls in pieces and the roof gone. The barn was nonexistent. Another casualty of war. I was pretty sure Zeke's property went untouched. I peaked at my native friend; my head tilted.

He understood the non-verbal question. "The Northern army burnt everything from the end of our land to the river.

Yours and your father's land are a casualty of war," he said as we approached the ruins.

He enquired again about my father, to which I responded to the best of my knowledge. "Yes, I guess the Union got him, but I'm not sure. Do you know what happened?"

He glanced around, watching the other members of the Coushatta, who stood watching the white man approach. All looked apprehensive about the event. They must have all witnessed my father's slaughter, or at least had intimate knowledge.

My father's associate interrupted, "They are not the ones who I want you to talk to. I wanted you to meet his parishioner, the Yank, who attended his service every week."

"With all due respect, I don't trust the white man. Most of these rebs and Yanks are on both sides. These Caddo are who I trust. I'd be dead if it weren't for them and Kat. We can go see him afterwards."

"As you wish." He shrugged.

My friend escorted me into the rubble of the old home, leaving my father's partner to stand outside, out of earshot, waiting as war surrounded us.

It was the two of us in the shanty.

"Robert, the man you're riding with is involved."

I stared at him, mouth ajar.

He continued. "He didn't kill him, but led your father to Cheneyville, where the US Calvary ambushed him. It was a Union Army from Louisiana."

"This man fights for the North?" I whispered, pointing towards the opening of the hut.

"It's rumored. Me and two of the men followed them down south past Alexandria. I saw him introduce your father to the Louisiana regiment. I could not hear what they were saying."

197

"They shot him?"

The young Caddo man rolled his eyes and sighed. "I'm getting there."

I tapped my fingers on the remains sitting on the mud floor. North winds whistled through the window.

"They left the makeshift fort, and he rode into the country where there was a battle between some confederate Louisiana troops and the First Calvary of Louisiana."

"So, it was a battle of Louisiana, New Orleans men fighting for the Union Army, and a bunch of bumpkins like myself fighting for our state?"

"Correct. Your father didn't see any action because they led him into some trenches. My brothers and I followed them. The man", he paused, crawled to the opening to peek out in search of my escort. He reentered to lead me to the far corner of the shack. "...rode off on his horse, leaving your father with the Unionists of Louisiana who beat them with a musket, then blindfolded him, before leading him to a tree where he faced a firing squad. We watched him take several bullets to the head. After they murdered your father, they tied him to his horse, and sent the animal galloping north into the waiting arms of Confederate soldiers. We cut through the bayous to witness the soldiers open fire on your father and his horse, killing the horse. Then we headed home, hopefully unnoticed."

"It doesn't make any sense. Why would they kill a man against slavery? I can see the true money makers, the Democrat elite, wanting him dead, since he opposed the war and the ideals of Louisiana, yet he loved this state like I do."

"Your father was an agitator, who preached against war and against slavery. He didn't want a war, but it's a moneymaker for the elite using these poor farm kids as pawns. Half these country boys do not know why or what they're fighting for. These boys aren't fighting to keep the slaves. They think they're fighting to defend their property. Where are you going?"

I crawled from the remains of the old home in search of the man I rode up with. The abolitionist traitor who set up my father. I also prepared to enlist in the Confederate Army and head to Cheneyville or New Orleans. Revenge was my motive. I tasted blood and wanted more.

Before I rode off, I whispered to my native friend, "Brother, I believe your story, so I'm going to ride with this man and kill him once he reveals the truth to me. Then I will seek the officers who did this to him. Like you said, most of these boys fighting the war are pawns in a game of chess, recruited to kill and sacrificed for the politicians and landowners. I am now one of them."

"Head back to Mexico, Robert. You have a wife with whom to grow a family together. Grow numbers in what you do. The more we create, the better off the world will be."

"Once my job is completed, I will return to Mexico and raise a family."

The young Caddo's glare told it all. "My brother, you are selfish. Risking your life to leave your wife a widow is not the answer. I've seen the posters. Some are still on storefront windows and nailed to pecan trees here. We remove them as soon as we see them posted. They do make good fire starters. You are wanted dead or alive. Confederates will take you out. The Union will take you out. Your family will take you out."

By the time he finished his soliloquy, I caught up with the man I rode from Texas with. "What took you so long, son?"

We had ridden through The Caddo land with my brothers on our trail, and then to meet parishioners. "I caught up with an old friend, a brother from another tribe. We grew up roping and riding together." I wasn't giving away anything,

Asking about Pa's and my home wouldn't be revealing what he knew about the slaughter of my father. I'd be curious to know if he knew anything. Plus, I needed him to begin talking.

"Northern Army came through this area a few months ago. Torched everything in their path. They took no prisoners. Your father wasn't home. He was in Alexandria. We were meeting with fellow abolitionists of Louisiana and East Texas on our role in the war."

No confession yet, but he put my father close to the action. He needed to keep speaking as we rode to Zeke's.

"What is our role? We can't be conscientious objectors in this. We must choose, and I want to protect my homeland first from the pillaging of the land. That's my priority."

"Mine too," he said without cracking.

I sought clues from the man on our way towards Coushatta seeking other friends of my father and then to seek Uncle Zeke. I wondered how he read me. Best I kept my gigantic trap shut.

We were both armed, me with a rifle, a handgun, and knives hidden. Missing was my trusty bullwhip, without which I felt naked. I had plenty of weapons in case this man tried attacking me, someone sought reward money, or Union or Confederate troops attacked.

The problem with war, and it happened down in Mexico, is that there are troops who flipped sides, soldiers who worked both sides, and with a war dividing families, this became a regular occurrence. My father trusted him, and he entrusted my life to him when journeyed to see him, however something besides the Caddo told me he wasn't to be trusted. It must have been a spiritual belief when we diverted paths at the beginning of our journey.

I watched the man sleep. He tossed and turned, clenched the pistol, and mumbled in his sleep. I tried making out the words, but they were unintelligible. We took turns standing guard. I slept with an eye open, monitoring him pace. If he wanted me dead, he could have taken me anytime. I was sure he wouldn't kill me but leading me into death became a possibility.

The next day we rode together, him leading as we headed towards Ezekiel Barnum's plantation. One of my father's favorite parishioners, also an abolitionist, lived about a mile west of the plantation.

"Robert," the man greeted me as we entered the small home. "You have questions about your father?"

"I do." I glanced towards my companion, who waited outside. "What do you know about it? I've heard different things."

My companion couldn't hear me because I spoke in a quiet manner. I glanced at the door, hoping this man and I were on the same page.

He led me to the back of the shanty, away from the front door. "Don 't travel with this man," he spoke in a soft tone. "Robert, you will meet your death sooner than later. Why did you think they sent you here to meet him?"

"What do you know?"

He repeated a similar story my Caddo brother told me, just not detailed since he didn't witness the slaying.

After he finished his version, he whispered, "Be careful with this man. He has ties to your Uncle Ezekiel."

We had one more stop, the plantation. I didn't want to go, but I had made it this far without being taken a prisoner or killed. I rode with danger, aware that this man who had set up my father, was also setting me up. He needed to be removed from life. I had to kill him, but after I met my uncle and my cousins.

We rode up on the plantation. The land was pure, no pillaging of the crops and pecan trees. If my deranged theory of war was correct, Zeke paid people off to keep people off his land. My father could not afford this luxury; thus, someone torched our land.

"Nephew Robert." The old chubby man came to greet me. His belly shook as he adjusted his suspenders. He stretched his arms, attempting to give me a hug.

I rebuked the idea and refused even a handshake.

"Robert, I am forgiving you for stealing my property. I lost my oldest son and my younger brother. You, Cletus and the girl are the only kin I have now. I no longer blame you for Josiah's death. Both you boys took a gigantic risk and knew your life would be in danger. I knew about his love for the piece of property he stole and that it would eventually happen. You, I didn't see it coming, and you stole my brightest girl. I had plans for her whether she complied."

"I'm glad I stole her then. She's a remarkable girl. Fighting for independence of Mexico. We wouldn't have made it without her."

"Remember, only two of you made it. I still had a slave and my eldest son died and you are back as a wanted man. I will not kill you. However, I can't protect you."

"Where's Clete?"

"He's down in Cheneyville, preparing to fight the traitors from New Orleans."

"I reckon I'll meet him down there after some unfinished business." I glanced at the man who had accompanied me from Texas. Zeke's eyes followed mine. The two older men acknowledged eye contact.

"Follow me." He put his arm around me and led me into the house. The man stayed outside. "He set your father up, and he's going to do it to you. Folks caught him harboring slaves right after you stole Kat."

"Cl..." I almost said my cousin's name. He knew our destination. He always played both sides, and he sought Kat for his mistress. I remained silent until I gathered my thought. "Someone knew about him turning the tables on all the operators, including my dad?"

My uncle grimaced and said nothing. His response answered my question without him answering.

"How should I do this?" I asked.

"Robert, the man set my brother up. My brother and I didn't agree on much on anything, we didn't speak either because the man wanted some damn equality. He didn't want war, so someone killing him, killed a little of myself. You need to get off my land since I don't want to deal with the evidence or the law. We're in a war and anything could have happened to him." He paused, lit a cigar and offered me one.

I accepted, standing on the porch outside his majestic plantation home. We stood there smoking until the man came over. Zeke handed him a smoke so that the three of us stood there enjoying the thick cigars, puffing smoke into the Louisiana sky. A sky that had seen smoke from cannon and musket fired way too often recently. The pleasant aroma of cigar smoke added an innocent ambience to the evening.

Zeke invited us to spend the evening. I refused the service of the slaves except for the cooking. Since living with Kat, I always made my plate and never expected her to serve me. We enjoyed a feast, which the soldiers who fought for this type of meal would never see. Ham, potatoes, and corn with a pecan pie for dessert. The man and I ate like it was our last meal, and for one of us, it might be.

Sleeping in a feather bed was also something I hadn't done in ages. Tossing and turning, I plotted to take this man out once we crossed the boundary of Zeke's land. I wanted him to tell me names, then his confession, and those would be his last words.

After a filling breakfast of biscuits and gravy with fried eggs, it was time to head out. The two of us rode out after giving my uncle our blessings. The end for one of us would be today. I remembered the land from years earlier. I also knew about the man and would seize my opportunity the first chance I got once we trotted from Zeke's land.

We meandered past the slave cabins, and I didn't recognize any of the help. Zeke must have restocked his workers after the great theft years earlier. I wanted to stop and chat, however butchering a traitor remained in my mind. I tipped my cap to the slaves sitting in their cabin, and also working in the trees, shaking down pecans.

I had spent my youth working with the enslaved, empowering them for revolutions and escapes. I felt at peace trotting through their quarters. It was part of my youth, which made me a man, something I felt proud of. Now a man, I was about to murder someone and blame it on war. Revenge is part of battle and Louisiana is in the thick of it.

I needed to enlist in Alexandria, a two-day horseback ride. I'd be riding alone or be dead. After exiting Zeke's plantation, we trotted along the Red River. The man and I scanned the landscape for the perfect spot. This was land I grew up on. I knew it like the back of my hand. I approached some Indian Mounds of the Coushatta and smiled as both horses galloped. He couldn't keep up.

I kicked the horse into the next gear and rode towards the mounds. If I got far enough ahead, I could attack. Uncle Zeke had handed me a new rope with which I could lasso him like a cow. By now I was familiar with the horse, and we soon rode like one. We meandered, cutting through tree lines and zigzagging around the mounds. The ridges were prominent, so staying between the hills saved time and energy. We cut through towards the last group of bluffs that kept me out of his vision.

Hitching the steed to a pecan tree near the Red River, I retraced my steps up the hill and waited with field glasses, watching for him. He rode close, not too far behind me. I sensed him gallop a separate path to sneak around the far side of the hill. My rope in hand to lasso him, I was ready to use my guerrilla training on him. If that failed, I'd shoot him. The man wouldn't make it five yards past the last hill.

He rode reluctantly through the ridges, the soil soggy and rough. A non-equestrian would have to be methodical while slashing through. The man couldn't ride. Again, the edge went to me. As he came closer, I twirled my wrist to spin and then flipped the rope. The man was less than twenty-five yards away. The rope circled around him. I yanked it tight enough to snag him off his horse. He tumbled across the savanna grass, failed to get a grip, somersaulting as I sprinted towards him with a rebel yell. I flashed the machete in his face.

He floundered on the ground, trembling, wriggling his arms in a futile attempt to squirm free. His eyes opened wider on realizing that his death was playing out right before his eyes. I would not disappoint his vision.

"Why are you doing this, Robert?" His speech was shaky. He knew his ultimate destiny.

"I should ask you the same question." My foot now stood across his throat; his floundering lessened with each passing moment. Any hesitation would cause extra pressure on his neck. "Why did you have my father killed?" That machete slashed his face. Blood erupted like geysers.

"Someone in your family betrayed me," he stuttered, head toward the mound and away from me.

My foot pressed harder on his throat. He gasped for air, his fingers struggling to lift my boot off his neck. I reduced the pressure to let him breathe and speak. "Who?"

"I-I-I don't know. Texas Rangers raided me."

"They made you turn in names?"

"Uh, huh."

"And you chose my father? Anyone one else?"

Silence.

"Anyone else?" I raised the blade, ready to decapitate the rat.

He continued his squelch without answering. The toe from my boot continued the pressure on his neck. My machete continued the puncturing.

"Who set you up?"

He gasped, struggling for words.

"Cousin," he struggled to spit out.

The machete descended on his throat, slitting the primary artery. Crimson fluid erupted like hot springs as it stained everything in its path. I had my answer and no longer needed the man. My cousin told the government about the underground railroad, and he turned in the conductors. My father and I were involved. He's dead, and I'm seeking revenge and leaving a trail of blood behind me.

I didn't enjoy the killing. It was revenge, not freedom fighting, not saving independence for the citizens down south who took me in. He turned my father in and me as well. For sure, the Louisiana Union Army would murder me once I met the real traitor. My cousin, Cletus.

Chapter 22

Eating squirrel and berries over the campfire south of Natchitoches became the perfect time to overthink. I never gave the rat a chance to say, your cousin, Cletus. What if it wasn't him? I had two cousins. I assumed Cletus, since he worked both ends on the way down. He was shifty, but what if he tried helping me? What if he tried to tell me something without ratting on his older brother? I always tossed him aside. What if it was Josiah and Cletus was innocent? The Mexican government had killed Josiah, but after my return to the states, I wasn't sure of anything anymore.

I had no way of verifying my doubts. I left Mexico with the thought that Zeke and Clete killed or had my father killed. My uncle seemed to be innocent. However, what about his son? I never suspected that the man we planned on staying with would set my father up. I thought about returning to Mexico, but the rat was nothing more than a setup man. Someone higher up, an elite in this war, wanted my father and me dead. It had to be the Union Army of Louisiana.

The next morning, I set out for Alexandria and penned Kat a letter. I had yet to write her since arriving back in the States.

The next evening, I reached Alexandria, a city along the Red River, which I followed and eventually enlisted as a private in the Confederate Army. I had no intention of defending the institution but sought only revenge for the death of my father. I needed the truth from my cousin. In my two-minute interview, I mentioned nothing about that. I informed them that I was a trained guerrilla fighter from the Mexican Army and had a cousin who I believed was a confederate soldier in Cheneyville. The gray coats accepted me right away, since they needed numbers to assist in the northern invasion. Since they weren't picky, they sent me to Fort DeRussy, a brief ride from the city. From inside the fort, I penned a letter to my wife.

DEAREST KAT.

MY STAY IN LOUISIANA WILL BE MUCH LONGER. I'VE ENLISTED IN THE CONFEDERATE ARMY. UNION TROOPS BASED OUT OF LOUISIANA KILLED MY FATHER. THEY SET HIM UP AS AN INSTIGATOR, A ROUSER, WHO DIDN'T WANT WAR. BOTH SIDES WANTED HIM SHOT. I'M NOT SURE YET IF MY UNCLE OR COUSIN CLETUS WERE INVOLVED, BUT WE KNOW CLETUS WORKED BOTH SIDES AND UNCLE EZEKIEL WAS A POWERFUL LANDOWNER WITH CONNECTIONS ON BOTH SIDES. WHILE SEARCHING FOR THE TRUTH, I THINK THEY WERE PART OF IT. I WILL RETURN ONCE JUSTICE IS DONE.

YOUR HUSBAND,

ROBERT

I wrote the letter in haste. To see the blood of the men who shot my father and accomplices to the murder became my desire. The struggles of Mexico between the French no longer mattered. I hoped for the best outcome and longed to see the Mexicans claim victory, but revenge outweighed the struggles from the nation that emancipated Kat and me.

A familiar lad paced back and forth in front of me, occasionally he glanced down, hoping to go unnoticed by me. Clete had grown into a tall, chiseled man, as if he worked the land himself instead of enslaving the labor. He exited the front where I sat writing to my bride, glanced over his shoulder and wiggled a finger for me to follow him. I glanced around to see if anyone else had noticed. Soldiers in gray scribbled notes in journals and letters to loved ones. No one else checked the surroundings as I chased my cousin down.

I went through three wooden doors before I came upon him. The room displayed isolation and desolation. No one else was there except the two of us, He wore a black hat atop his uniform. My cousin whittled an arrow from a stick, his eyes fixed on me as I approached. Neither of us spoke for a minute.

He reached into the torn shirt pocket and whipped out a chunk of tobacco, which he slit with his whittling knife, plopped it in his mouth and chawed on it for a few minutes. He spat black juice on the ground.

"You're still alive. What brings you here to fight with us, Rebs?"

I remained across the room from him, refusing to flinch. "Revenge. When the men who killed my father are all gone, I'll return to Mexico. That includes whoever set him up. One is already gator food."

Clete's expression gave nothing away. We had escaped despite his working on every side. He played both sides perfectly. He was a shifty kid when I last saw him but was now a calculating young man. The stare down continued, giving me time to calculate my strategy.

He spoke after a brief silence. "You think I killed your pa? I don't kill kinfolk and don't have them killed." Nothing in his face said he was lying, then again, this kid was a born liar, probably never told the truth. He was now a soldier. Honesty was the last thing on a soldier's mind. Protecting yourself and your brothers in arms came first.

"Whoever set up Will Harris in Texas, set up my father. You snuck ahead of us and knew the locations. Will set up my father in order for the First Calvary to do him in. I know this already."

He glanced away for a split second, but it was a brief second too long. He showed his hand.

I continued. "Guess where Will Harris is now?"

The bright blue eyes met mine. "Dead?"

"On the southern end of the mounds, south of Zeke's land. Unless gators hauled him away or the army trapesing through discovered his headless corpse."

"You peace loving Quaker, you killed him?" He squinted, a smile forming on his stoic face.

"I'm a veteran of the Mexican Army. I killed lots of Frenchmen for no reason except that they invaded my adopted country." The knife was soon on display, blade pointed at my cousin. "I ain't afraid to use this either. Military issue."

"You ain't no soldier. You couldn't hit the broad side of the barn with a rifle."

I took two steps towards him. "Don't need no guns, since I'm a guerrilla fighter and do my best work up close." I took another step closer.

He drew back. I had total control but was not ready to kill. I needed answers. The edge he thought he had on me now dissipated.

"What do you need me to do?"

There was an untrusting twinkle in his eye. I needed to earn his trust. Combat was the primary way.

"They need scouts, don't they? Let's go check the river for bluebellies," I said.

"You're on the wrong side of the war. Bluebellies want to free the slaves, "he replied.

"Those troops don't give a damn about Kat, Millie, or anyone else. They just doing what Sherman, Grant, and Lincoln tell them to do. Savage our land, slaughter the people. Have you seen Pa's land? Ain't nothing left. Somehow, Zeke's plantation is fine. By the way, you helped them escape. Why are you fighting?"

"I want to keep the Yanks out of Louisiana, same as you."

"Then let's ride out and look for the Calvary. I'm ready for revenge."

We rode out at night. I had never been this far South in Louisiana. The bayou was thicker, the wildlife more abundant with snakes and gators roaming the swamp. We both felt at home. I wanted one name from him, and I was sure he'd give it to me. I would not spare him. His flinching was a confession, and I was ninety-nine per-cent sure he turned Mr. Harris in. I needed a confession from my cousin. Clete needed to see what I could do. We waited in the bayou for the Calvary. Previous scouting activity had them close, south of Marksville, near Simmesport.

We approached the area and noticed Union troops.

"There they are," Clete whispered. "The First Union Calvary of Louisiana. Got troops working both sides."

"How do you know?"

My cousin glared at me. Another correct assumption on my part.

"Cover me," I called out, dismounting at the same time. I snuck into the forest in search of the soldier who wandered off. Armed with my knife, machete, rope and rifle, I snuck through cypress trees, not caring about reptiles.

A young, unsuspecting kid about sixteen sauntered towards me. He appeared disoriented as most troops who sometimes indulged in local moonshine or wild plants grown down here. Unaware of my presence, he took a few steps by me, when I put the machete to his throat, kicked him to the ground and tied him up. I dragged him through the swamp to meet my cousin, where he would soon be our prisoner.

Scratches and cuts covered his body when I showed up to where we hid. "I got it in me to do more. Let's make him talk, then take him to the captain and let him decide."

"Kill him now. You're the guerrilla who bragged about snagging some lost soldier and slashing his throat. Do it. Remember, there is still a reward for your head."

"I want to make him talk. I'm sure his commander knows something. Help me flop the kid on my horse."

We struggled to lift the boy without caring if we dropped him. A fall only added more scratches to his pimpled face. He hung limp over the tail of my steed, flailing in back of the saddle.

Clete mounted his horse. I walked towards mine and put my foot in the stirrup.

"Wait!" he shouted, his revolver aimed at the boy and the horse.

I rode. He shot the kid in cold blood several times, and the boy fell into the mud. My horse galloped off into the unknown as Clete followed, leaving me with no supplies, no ride and a dead Union soldier. I had my weapons, and I'd use them if needed.

The erupting gunfire woke up troops who camped nearby. I heard commotion over the critters living in the swamp. The voices grew louder as I skedaddled on foot, making my way through the bayou, the same way I entered. My rope was in use with a tied up, pimple faced, red head boy who might have been fifteen laid on the ground.

Surrendering was not an option. I didn't make it far, zigzagging through the swamps. Sitting on his horse was Commander Harai Robinson.

"Here is an enemy of the United States. A traitor, a criminal wanted for theft of personal property, who fought for the enemy of the United States and a boy who fled the country."

I wondered how a man I never seen before, and never knew existed, knew so much about me.

Another soldier rode up, flashing his pistols. It was Clete. Two more officers arrived on horseback. "I told you you'd meet the men who killed your father. Meet Captains Cheney and Jones."

They pointed their weapons at me, when I tried to reach for mine.

My instincts yelled to fire. John the Caddo mentioned something about a Cheney or was it Cheneyville. I grabbed my weapon, wrapped my fingers around the pearl handle, index finger on the trigger and pulled the revolver from the holster. Captain Cheney dropped as soon as I fired. Clete disappeared, never to be heard from again, while the other captain arrested me after swinging the butt of his rifle against my temple.

"Your hide is worth more alive than full of holes," he told me as more troops hauled me to their fort.

I was in no position to be brash, but I knew I would only see daylight the moments before my public execution. "Which one of you killed my father?" I asked Jones, ignoring the biting pain of my hands knotted behind my back as we rode the train to New Orleans.

Jones pondered the question, which meant he had information. He scratched his head. "You want to know if you avenged your father's death before you're dropped in the gallows?"

213

I nodded, afraid to speak anymore. I peered into Jones's eyes just before he threw a hood over my face.

"You got one of them, the other vanished before our eyes tonight. I'll tell you the story on the ride down." He continued. "Your father was a conscientious objector to the war, which in the US Army made him a traitor to the Union cause. We had a mission to round up anyone who opposed the Union involvement, including anyone against the war. We received a tip. Cheney and Cletus Barnum took him to Cheneyville. Cletus was used because your father trusted his nephew."

I grunted, and got my head smashed by the butt of his gun. I came to in New Orleans's cell. Untied and demasked, I sat on a bench in the dark, scheduled to be hung in a week.

The week was too long. I penned a letter to Kat, informing her of my execution. I wanted to inform her myself, rather than hear it from the government in a letter she may or may not receive.

I wished now they would have killed me right there. I wished Cletus would have a put the bullet through my brain. He lived a long life knowing he murdered his only cousin. If there was to be a Barnum ancestor, I prayed they acted on the other side of the family and took Cletus Barnum out before he bred. The bastard was impregnating slave girls he aided in escape.

Waiting to die is a tough thing, especially knowing the date and time, and how. I wanted them to do it in a timely fashion. Psalms my father and Zeke forced into my head came racing back in the dark. I blurted out Psalm 23:4. *"Even though I walk through the valley of the shadow of death, I fear no evil, for You are with me; Your rod and Your staff, they comfort me."*

They charged me with the murder of Captain Cheney, Will Harris, and the theft of Ezekiel Barnum's property. The reward money would go to Uncle Zeke since he originally posted it. I wanted to believe my family's innocence in this. Zeke owned people, but most Southern landowners did, it made them guilty of a racist exploiter of humans, however it was also the way of life in prewar Louisiana. Cletus was capable of anything, and I wouldn't put it past him, including murdering his kin. I now understood why my father was assassinated. Clete and his father knew I'd return, and my execution would be inevitable. I pondered my life for the rest of the week.

I would be the only one hung that day.

Chapter 23

Cletus Barnum.

I watched my cousin, the kid who tried to kill me, being hauled out. Troops from both sides of the war watched the traitorous young man being led to his death, his legs shackled, and hands cuffed behind his back. His side of the family would go extinct, no more peace-seeking abolitionist-thinking Barnums in the world. I needed to see this impostor flop to his death and witness his neck snap in half up close, but they could no longer see me in public as I hid near the river in a grove of bald cypress trees. The riverboat waited for me, hauling troops up the Mississippi River. I wasn't the only one wanting to see his neck crack. Robert was the only hanging scheduled, so I watched from outside the Fort with my field glasses rested on my nose.

Robert staggered out with his hands tied behind him. His legs chained together as he dragged them across the scaffolding. He could see everything and what would happen to him. At the gallows, he slipped his ugly mug through the tied noose.

Atop my horse, I lit a cigar. I grinned as the hangman slipped the noose over his head. The crowd applauded and yelled. They loved successful lynching in this neck of the woods.

"Take your time. Make the traitor suffer," voices screamed from the gallery.

I won't mention what slurs others yelled; however, I had no problem with what they called the treasonous thief. The crowd applauded louder when they tossed the hood over his head.

"Any last requests?"

"Let my wife know I love her, and always will."

"We will notify your wife of your passing through the US Army, which is all we can do," the hangman said through the cone-shaped device, allowing the spectators to hear every word.

They hoisted Robert with a rope which strangled him. They pulled the lever adjacent to where Robert swung, then the floor released as he descended towards the ground. The crowd applauded the moment his head snapped like the beans they grew. I just puffed at my cigar and rode off, aware that I was also a wanted man. So far, I have helped several slaves escape and sired several children, and one day I'd be free. As of now, I left New Orleans on a riverboat, a joyous man. My destination was Texas and deserting the Confederacy. I needed to create an alias. Clarence Bourgeois would be born. Cletus Barnum would no longer exist.

Part III

Chapter 24

Kat Barnum

San Luis Potosi, Mexico

Since Mexico City fell to the French in 1863, President Benito Juarez remained in power, though he remained at large. Juarez moved the capital 300 miles to the north to San Luis Potosi. I continued to be a soldadera in the Mexican Army, however my body didn't feel like fighting.

The locals, the freed slaves and the Indigenous all spoke with me. They knew what was going on. I carried Robert's baby and wrote a letter informing him that he was going to be a father. I wondered how long it took for them to receive the communication.

I hadn't received a letter from him in ages, but then again, we lived in separate countries that were both knee-deep in bloodshed. One of them battled with itself, while my new homeland fought French invaders who now ruled the country. We fled Puebla and Mexico City to Central Mexico. I missed Robert but wasn't worried about him, only a tad impatient awaiting a telegraph, something, anything, from him.

My fellow female soldaderas took care of me, making sure I didn't over-exert myself. Then again, I didn't know any different. My entire life, I had worked with everything I had, from picking pecans, cotton and other crops off of master's land, and also being a domestic for Ezekiel Barnum. I stayed put in the new capital and aided the Army.

In the spring of 1864, I received my first letter from Robert. He remembered to date it, at least.

DEAREST KAT.

MY STAY IN LOUISIANA WILL BE MUCH LONGER. I'VE ENLISTED IN THE CONFEDERATE ARMY. UNION TROOPS BASED OUT OF LOUISIANA KILLED MY FATHER. THEY SET HIM UP AS AN INSTIGATOR, A ROUSER WHO DIDN'T WANT WAR. BOTH SIDES WANTED HIM SHOT. CLETUS WORKED BOTH SIDES AND UNCLE EZEKIEL WAS A POWERFUL LANDOWNER WITH CONNECTIONS ON BOTH SIDES. I THINK THEY WERE PART OF IT AND I'M SEARCHING FOR THE TRUTH. ONCE JUSTICE IS DONE, I WILL RETURN.

YOUR LOVING HUSBAND,

ROBERT

His letter left me more hopeless. It was three months since he wrote it and he had not found me. True, our band of soldiers and soldaderas were on the run. Robert was resourceful. He knew where to ask for information. Anyone up in the Northern part of the country would help. I feared for him. Louisiana had to be a far more dangerous place right now. In Mexico, the men protected us, but if the fighters wandered too far from the capital, we might be in trouble. As of now, we regrouped and planned counter attacks.

Guerrilla fighting still prevailed further north Tampico near the town Robert and I originally settled. It was due east of San Luis Potosi around two-hundred-seventy miles. The capital sat inland in the mountainous area, while Tampico lay on the coast.

I went with a few other soldaderas, accompanying male guerrilla fighters, to kill French soldiers in the Northeastern port city. Four months pregnant now, I wanted to join my fellow women and male freedom fighters once again seeking independence. Being pregnant, leaders would not let me. I had only heard from Robert on the one letter, but then again, we vagabonded from a new capital city to new headquarters anytime President Juarez felt threatened.

Other soldiers told me part of the threat was internal. Morale became low as I volunteered to help the guerrillas.

"You cannot go," the commander in charge told me. It's too risky especially for a pregnant woman.

I didn't care about my baby; I didn't care about myself. Without Robert, I felt nothing, no companion and no strength. All I had was my internal grit and spirit, who refused me to stop. "I'm going. The baby won't slow me down but give me extra strength."

"You may lose your baby," he communicated in Spanish.

I responded in Spanish. I had learned the language hanging with soldaderas the last three years.

"I don't care. My husband is gone, and I've written over and over and had not heard back. Soldiers are deserting the army, only to wind up fighting against us. I'm desperate, and I need to help in every way I can. You gave Robert and me freedom, but now I must give your country freedom from the French." I smeared mud on my face to camouflage myself, threw a knife into a pine-oak tree so the blade stuck in the bark. I yanked the knife out of the tree, collected sticks which I shaved into spears with the glowing edge of the knife. After scouting the forest, I spotted a kit fox. The stringed stick I used as a bow was already on my back. I held the tip of the homemade arrow against the string. The fox rolled on the ground after I pulled back and aimed. I decided that I'd cook it for the soldiers later.

The commander watched the coldness with which I killed the petite mammal, admiring the way I handled myself. Again, in Spanish, he told me, "You're resourceful, can shoot, toss a knife and fearless. We need soldiers and soldaderas like you to take charge." He exhaled and continued. "I need you to lead a band of men and women guerrillas to Tamaulipas to the coast if needed and take out as many French and French sympathizers as possible." He pinned a star on me, showing authority. "Senora Barnum, are you ready for this authority?"

"Yes, sir." I saluted the man and clicked the heels of my boots.

He escorted me to a band of twenty other commandos. Some of them were women, most were men, all of assorted heritage. Escaped slaves, Indigenous and Mexicans all stood to salute me when I approached them by a small campfire.

Again, he addressed the troops in his native tongue. "At ease. This is Senora Katerina Barnum. She will lead you to the coast. Since Senora Barnum joined our cause, she has worked as a cook, a scout and fighter. She escaped slavery in the United States of America and has shown a needed coldness to her oppressors. She has been a valued fighter for the Mexican people and all the underground fighters. Viva Mexico."

"Viva Mexico," my troops responded in unison, raising their weapons with their right arms. Most carried spears, knives, machetes, or a combination of two or all three.

Two men, both freed slaves, were the muscle of my outfit. Two Mexican soldiers carried the rifles for distant kill or rescue. Our mission was to attack, intimidate the French, and drive them out of our country. Our mission might be treacherous, but the land to the coast needed to be conquered. The Port of Tampico needed reopened so we could receive weapons from our foreign allies.

Our training included riding as one. As a young girl admiring Robert take-charge of the four of us, his smile had stuck. I snuck a peek back at the men and woman riding with me. My confident grin shone through the high desert night even as I gouged the horse's kidneys with my spurs. The black three-year-old trotted off through the vegetation in the high desert.

We rode as one unit with the snipers bringing up the rear. They had their orders to fire if needed. Two men taking on the role of my strength rode with me. The fully armed men carried rifles, pistols, knifes and machetes. The rest of my troop had on them carved spears, bows, arrows and machetes and knives but no guns. I carried the same equipment as the guerrillas, but fully armed with a rifle and pistol. No one was going to stop my quest for freedom. Only my suicidal self.

The ride to the valley would be a three-day venture. There was no timeline, but the faster we went to the valley, the quicker we'd pillage the French stronghold. Wasting time was not an option, neither was riding in haste. The unit became efficient as we switched from a mountainous high-desert terrain into the rain forest, and then down the treacherous slopes into the valley.

I'd love to commemorate Robert for his leadership and team building, but I could not. Robert and his cousin Josiah spent too much time bickering to be in charge. My team building skill came from Josiah and Cletus's father, Ezekiel, the slave-master and head of the plantation. The man always preached about working together, growing together. As a slave, becoming efficient meant more profit for Ezekiel. I assumed it would work in battle.

On the third day of our ride, a freed woman slave named Sara accosted me. "Why you in charge, anyway?"

"Commander chose me, because I don't care. We're on a mission to take back our port and we'll stop at nothing. They chose you because of your strengths, and so was I."

"You're the pregnant one, ain't ya? You should be back at the fort protecting your baby."

I looked at her like she's a fool. "Why protect my baby if my baby can't live free? For you and me, this is our first freedom, and we have an opportunity to fight for it. I don't want my baby fighting for her freedom, so I'm going to give it to her. I can feel her already and this kid got some spirit with her. The baby gonna lead the way."

The girl, who might have been eighteen, came from East Texas, near Beaumont, possibly related to that old man looked up at me, smiling. "Spirits come through many sources. Robert is a white man, they all say?"

"Yes, he is. Why do you ask?"

"He a believer?"

"His daddy was a pastor, and uncle was too."

"That's not what I meant. He believes in Hoodoo. You know if he did, that baby gonna be special. If he is not a believer, the baby just your baby. She ain't gonna have the powers."

I wasn't a staunch believer in the magic. Ezekiel Barnum was a good preacher, and I started following the white man's religion while enslaved. The ones that came from Texas believed in the magic, but I wasn't sure. Robert once told me that I had to believe 100 percent in the religion for it to work. I didn't fully believe in the white man's religion, neither his father's version nor his uncle's. The Hoodoo from the Caribbean and different tribes of West Africa were also something different. On this mission, I sought assistance from my young soldier.

In her, I saw my reflection from years earlier when an older white boy stole me off his kinfolks plantation and we never looked back. Her name was Sara, a pretty girl. I wanted to believe her magic. She rode with me. For this mission to

226

be successful, we needed all the spiritual guidance we could muster.

The third day towards the coast, I let her ride with me and the two freedmen I considered my muscle and enforcers. I treasured having them ride behind me. Like me, they had nothing to lose and treasured their freedom, so they'd do anything to remain free men. Muscular and armed to the bone, the two were perfect for their assigned role.

The rest loped behind us as we made a descent into the valley. I did not expect any action for a few days, since the commander briefed before departing. But this was war, so once we went hard towards the valley, anything could happen. I slowed the crew down; better observance was required descending the slopes.

Wildlife from the thick rainforest startled us. Pumas wandered the basin alongside big cats, so it was best to spot them first. The enforcers and snipers were ready to fire. Snakes slithered through the descending trails. They needed only one bullet to eliminate the reptile if needed. Again, my men remained ready.

The Indigenous knew this land. I wanted one to step up and help lead, so I chose a thirty-five-year-old male from the local Huasteco tribe, whose Spanish was worse than mine. However, he rode with a translator who kept me informed.

Words, which sounded like gibberish, rang out behind me. The Huasteco man heard something, and in a flash, two men spoke the same drivel.

"Alto," the translator spoke in Spanish.

We all stopped as he proceeded towards me. "Hay hombres en estas colinas."

"There are men in these hills," I translated to the escapees.

The men scoped the area. Sara closed her eyes in prayer, while the rest waited for the leader to decide.

I glanced at Sara at the end of her quick meditation. The snipers had caught up, gathering us in a circle. Both natives spoke to one another, then the translator approached me. All communication was in Spanish.

I spoke to my enforcers and Sara in English once we gathered closer. "French guerrillas are in the hills." Though my eyes focused on the three, most of my attention remained on the young girl. I needed her spiritual guidance. Fire burned in her eyes. The look she gave me reminded me of the healers my relatives spoke of in the quarters of Master Ezekiel's plantation. I motioned with my head towards the noise. Sara grinned in acknowledgement of my decision.

The other members of my guerrillas gathered. I despised using pawns since they cast me less than the chess piece. The band of commandos slipped into the forest, where the Huasteco had heard the rustling. Indigenous led the way, a bravery that encouraged the rest of the crew to follow. I watched the camouflaged warriors silently slip deep into the forest. They were so quiet that I didn't see or hear them as I slipped in, followed by the enforcers.

The French guerrillas never had a chance even though they waited for the onslaught. We shot their fighters from trees, our aims so accurate that bodies soon flopped to the ground. To ensure that there were no survivors, my group slit French throats and bludgeoned chests with machetes.

Our snipers shot those cowards who ran in the back. Twenty-three of their guerrillas lay dead, while we had zero casualties. I had won my first battle as a commander, a pregnant former slave, however our job only began. Our mission was to clear out the French to the coast, the first place I lived, and that was Tampico.

We continued the pillaging heading toward the coast. We rode another two days before any sign of the enemy, then traces began to turn up. They carelessly left campfires partially extinguished. Coals embered in vacant patches of land.

I called to my scouts, the Huastecos, to search the area with my enforcers. My troops and I followed them into the jungle, where our mud packed bodies blended with the vegetation. The scouts found a group of about twenty, whose mission was to wipe out the Mexican guerrilla fighter bands like us. They never got the chance.

Everyone knew their role as we slit throats open so that European blood spurt into the mud and merged with the rainforest. Ruthless and savage, we didn't care, and had nothing to lose. Although neutral, I was told by Robert as well as the commanders at camp that the French supported the Confederacy and the institution which enslaved me. I wanted them out of Mexico and dreaded going back to the institution which owned Millie, Sara, my enforcers, and all our families. It was the institution which Robert stole me from. My relentless commanding continued with my crew loving every annihilation they gave the intruders. Nineteen more French lay dead by the time we were done tossing the bodies. I wanted to torch them but assumed the wildcats and crocodiles which frequented the hills and swampy valleys needed quick meals. So, we left the carcasses for the scavengers and rode towards Tampico.

We rode in the valley, making our way across the coastal plain, past guerrillas that fought in the swamps and rainforests. A division of the Mexican Army was to meet us in the city by the end of the week. They had two days. I was ready for more killing and destruction. So were my troops.

The trek towards town took two uneventful days. The Mexican Army rested outside of town. Our mission was to raid the French camp, send them into a frenzy, and have them chase us towards the army. Both divisions camped on the edge of Tampico, since French troops occupied the city.

We maneuvered to the south end of the village, leaving the army to stay north. Nightfall met up sitting around the fire.

"Captain," Sara said to me. "Something ain't right."

I trusted her for my decisions. She didn't need to say a word, since I read her like a book. "What is it?" My words were soft, as not to arouse my crew.

"We're being set up." She gazed into the fire, searching for her intervention.

I had never questioned her in the past and relished the role she and I played in our domination. "Go on."

She glanced at the others, who were out of hearing distance, as long as we kept the tone to a whisper. "General Diaz is in charge. He appointed these men. Diaz and Juarez have different points of view and I heard this from others in our group."

I interjected. "So, we're going to do our raid, take out a handful of troops and flee."

"Yes."

"Then run towards the Army, where they will take over."

"They're not taking over. It's a setup." Sara's voice was barely above a whisper.

"We can't abort the mission, not now."

"If we follow proper instructions, it will be every person for themselves, plus they filled the division with traitors to our cause."

"We don't have a cause. This is an adopted country. I'm not being a scapegoat for their independence. If I'm fighting for it, I'm going to win," I said louder than I wanted.

"What are you saying?"

"I have a new plan."

Our conversation was still in whispers. Her wide eyes asked the question.

"One or two of us will enter the city and it will be a dangerous mission. They may not return." Her eyes widened. "French troops would follow them to where the Mexican Army awaits. Meanwhile, the rest of us set up an ambush. We're guerrillas, we don't have the strength or numbers of either army, however we always have the element of surprise."

"I'll take Jameson with me." Jameson was one of my enforcers. I didn't want either of them to go.

"You guys aren't...."

"No, Kat, this ain't our war. I know the regimen is a mess. The captain is a Diaz man. Take him out and the division will fall apart."

I grinned. "He's mine then. They sent him to kill me."

Chapter 25

Flames from our fire climbed into the warm night sky. The shadows enveloped her face, making my grin to widen. The flickering flame made me think about speaking spirits. The flame spoke about the man who Mil and Josiah sacrificed their souls for, so Robert and I would make it. Sara spoke the same language as Millie and the man from Beaumont, a language I understood, but didn't always comprehend.

Jameson and Sara took off into the night, while the howls of wolves and coyotes echoed in the Mexican night. Then it hit me. They were both on a suicide mission, so the rest of us could survive. I lost two friends this way and would not lose two more. My renegades were going to get some rest, none were aware of my change of plans. I'd inform them in the morning.

The sun rose over the city we were supposed to capture. My cook prepared a light meal with fruit and cooked critter. I addressed my group over breakfast.

"Intelligence states we're here to be set up. General Diaz wants a Mexican Army not indigenous people from Mexico. He does not want the escaped slaves from the United States. There are several of us renegades in this group, and Captain Fuentes wants us dead. We're being set up by our own army." I looked over at my tired troops and continued making up a speech. "Jameson and Sara rode into town to rile up the enemy. Our mission is to take on our Army. They will certainly look for us riding from town. Captain Fuentes is mine. We take out whoever defends him.

"What about the French?" one of the Mexicans asked.

"I don't care about them. Right now, my worry is our own army. Another regiment will take the city back."

We rode off, taking care to stay hidden. Our faces and bodies were mud packed. Our clothes blended with the camouflage. We rode near the Army and hitched up the horses. Then we snuck outside the Army, remained hidden and waited. With any luck, Jameson and Sara would sprint by with the French Army on their tail and the confusion would give us renegades an edge.

It didn't take long before I heard Sara's hollers, her legs kicking her horse into a frenzy. Jameson followed close behind her. My eyes darted round the perimeter, but no French soldier followed. I saw Captain Fuentes go after Sara and I sprinted towards him, wielding my machete with both hands. I nailed him in the throat, but not before he shot off a couple of rounds. Both crews exchanged gunfire, and others slashed and received deep cuts.

Sara's horse kept riding without faltering. She clung to the reins like her life depended on it. Three members of the brigade shot Jameson before he could make it out of the camp. I rode after Sara with the reminiscence of my commandos. It was almost difficult to catch up with her riding hard. I tailed her, riding like Robert taught me. I didn't care about the rest, since my mind was set on only Sara. Seven survivors of the massacre struggled to keep pace. Leaving them in the dust wasn't my choice, however survival was, as bullets whizzed by.

I caught up with Sara, she spoke to me as our horses sprinted through the forest. "I was right about them, wasn't I?"

"Yes, and I got Fuentes."

"He missed me, I'm sure, but let's keep moving."

I noticed a couple of crimson stains dripping from her arm. She was lucky they were not near an organ. We continued through the forest; the others lagged further behind. It was while we splashed through a river that I noticed the flourishing stain.

"Sara, we need to treat your arm. Blood is gushing."

"I'm fine. We need to get further away."

Robert had pulled this move before. I had watched him with Josiah. Sara pulled ahead not ready to take the bleeding seriously. Picking up the pace, I stood in the stirrups stroking the beast then I took the leap. I landed on her brown and white speckled pony, steadied myself and yanked. We tumbled across the mud, our bodies somersaulting together as we rolled a few times.

The horses had quit running. I picked her up to treat her wound. The penetration was above her elbow, right next to her bicep. I ripped my headscarf off my noggin and slit her sleeve with my knife-blade. Near her shoulder, I tied my scarf around her arm tight enough to stop blood from exiting her wound. I wandered parts of the forest seeking healing plants to slow the spread of infections. We were near Huasteco territory. What I gathered was that they were nomadic, wandering from the hills to the coast. We didn't spot any of them on our way to Tampico, and I direly needed them now.

I gathered the horses, put Sara in front of mine, and together we rode deep into the jungles, searching out locals. With the delay, my group caught up with no one tailing them. My Huasteco guide led me deep into the forest in search of an Indigenous village. His village. We wondered into a forest of thick pine-oak trees and came to a clearing, where a thriving community of Mexican natives sat. They greeted my guide with bows, showing respect. He explained in a local language who we were and what happened to Sara, and soon they took the girl away.

In Spanish, he told me the area was stocked with .traditional herbs to treat infections. She will be fine. I trusted the man. He was one who sided with Sara on the sabotage we faced. He also saved my life.

During our stay in the rainforest, the natives served the seven survivors local meals comprising tortillas from maze, papayas, and other plants. The healer of the tribe took care of us, with Sara spending hours in their care, and having a bullet removed from her arm, then stealing her soul. Herbs, live branches, live chickens and eggs were placed on Sara's arm in front of the effigies of Catholic Saints to conclude her healing. I overheard the faint prayers spoken in Spanish. We spent three nights in the village enjoying more traditional meals before leaving.

Slipping out single file from the back of the village with my guide leading the way, Sara and I trailed the group. This was virgin territory for us, and we needed to stick together. We had no idea what our plan was after returning upstate, but we had time to figure it out.

I looked forward to my promotion, but after the sabotage at Tampico, a public execution might be in order. Desertion seemed to be the best bet, especially since Mexico was a large country. There were plenty of places to hide.

Arriving at a clearing, I rode up adjacent to my guide. "Why can't we stay with your people?"

Again, he spoke in Spanish. "I don't want to put my village in jeopardy." He looked at me, his gaze accusing me of wanting to jeopardize his clan.

"Are there any safe nearby villages? Places that will accommodate a ragtag team of Mexican soldiers looking to escape the war?"

The man smiled. "Let me lead but stay close behind."

We followed him to a brotherhood village of his tribe. There he walked over to have a word with a man. They used animated hand signs before my guide jumped on his stallion, kicked its kidneys and fled on horseback. All we saw was the horse's rear hooves kicking up the mud, sprinting through the terrain.

The rest of us stood, waiting as Mexican troops surrounded us. They were led by the survivors of Captain Fuentes's traitorous soldiers. The captain's assistant, a young officer, who wore spectacles pointed at me.

"She was the leader of the troop, the one who bludgeoned Captain Fuentes with her machete."

They arrested me alongside the others, who were only following orders and did not deserve the punishment coming to them. They returned all of us to the capital city with our wrists roped behind our backs so tight that it threatened to cut off our circulation. The trip on horseback took seven days that turned out to be a week of misery. They loosened the ropes only when it was time to relieve ourselves with a guard watching me, and to eat our meal once a day. Sara got the same treatment as I.

I was relieved when we finally ended in the capital. President Juarez's men met us and talked individually to each of us in private.

I met with Senor Juarez privately. "Senora Barnum. Did you kill Captain Fuentes?"

"Yes, I did," I answered proudly, standing tall with direct eye contact.

"Why did you kill him?"

"His men killed one of my best men and planned an ambush on us. Captain Fuentes was one of Diaz's top aides. For the ultimate mission, they planned on killing all of us."

"Where did you hear this from?"

"I don't like revealing my sources in fear of what will happen to them. All my troops were following orders and—"

"The people under your command will go unpunished and receive only a dishonorable discharge, but free to leave the army. All but one, your wounded top assistant. The woman who looks like you. I've heard she was your top aide and advisor."

"What is going to happen to her?" I asked, revealing my source.

"My top aide is in conversation with her. Your fate is with her right now."

The president left the room, leaving me sitting with my face between my knees, nauseous and tired. The battle took a month, and I entered my second trimester of pregnancy. Footsteps pounded outside; voices mumbled as I stood to find a safe space to vomit. Returning to where I squatted, an aide of President Juarez hurried through the opening to the room.

"Senora Barnum." He cleared his throat. "I have good news for you. We will spare your life. Your aide confessed she told you about a possible ambush, but the fact you are pregnant means they will not hang you. You will spend the next two years imprisoned here."

I tried to stand to salute the officer. My body remained weak and nauseous. I fainted but remained fully aware. My speech slurred as I attempted to speak.

The officer noticed my struggle. "Remain seated, Senora. Please ask your question."

I asked in Spanish. "What is going to happen to my aide?"

He looked at me with sad eyes. "Sara, your aide will face the ultimate penalty. We will hang her this Friday."

Today was Tuesday.

"Can I speak with her?"

"Of course, you can." He spoke in Spanish.

On Thursday, they escorted me to her private cell made from adobe. Her quarters were small with minuscule room to maneuver. Her face illuminated like a lantern when she spotted me.

I crouched and crawled through the passageway that led into her cell. Tears welled in my eyes. "I've been trying to have your name cleared. You were following orders, not from me, but from a higher order," I said.

"Kat, I'm doing this to save your life. They don't care if you're with child. The government doesn't care they set us up for an ambush. All of this was true, and they know that. You'd be hung too...."

I interrupted. "You sacrificed your life for me?" The inflection asked a question, but it was more of a statement.

She burrowed her head between her knees, afraid to look me in the eye. Her response told me the truth she was afraid to say. We stood in silence, with Sara refusing to make eye contact. After a while, she glanced at me with tears cascading her face.

"I had to, Kat. You have a husband and a baby on the way and soon your family will reunite. I got nothing, just Jameson who chased me around, but he chased everything, and I wasn't gonna lay down with him, since he laid with numerous others."

"I ain't heard from Robert for months. I got his baby but he don't know that. He was long gone before I found out."

"I'm sure he's fine. A man fighting for his daddy should be protected." She stopped in mid-thought and buried her head again between her knees.

"Sara, what is it?"

The only sound she made was the sniffling accompanying the descending tears. Sara lifted her head, her nose dripping mucus. She continued to sob, but through the tears, I made out her chant. "I didn't ask for protection for him. I'm so sorry, Kat."

I didn't know what she meant, perhaps some old African spirits haunted and guided this journey. I never believed in them, but Millie and Sara did. Millie was dead, and Sara was set to be hung. At dawn, she will give her life. Both women gave their life for me. I had to find the man they sacrificed themselves to.

I crawled to Sara. "I will do everything I can to spare your life. Everything."

"You can't. This is my fate. You don't mess with fate, you gonna screw yourself."

"How do I talk to this thing?"

"He needs gifts, Kat, give him whiskey, some smokes, all the devil's work."

"You dealing with the devil?"

Footsteps came from down the hall. A guard escorted me away before Sara could answer.

I looked at her with teary eyes. "I will never forget you."

The guard steered me to my cell. Even though her hanging would be public, I never saw her again.

The next day, I sat alone in my cell. It was time for her execution; however, I refused attending. It exhausted me, especially with a new life growing inside me. Movement came from my abdomen to match the applause echoing throughout the fort. They lynched Sara from the Mexican army, and I felt the movement of my child. Changes in me needed to be made, but I also sought protection for me and my unborn child.

Chapter 26

Two months after the Sara's lynching, they took me to the infirmary. An amateur medical staff, consisting of a mid-wife and a physician, performed the delivery. I was now a mother of a beautiful daughter.

I stayed imprisoned for most of the war up north. My daughter was born incarcerated; however, my imprisonment was not strict. I had privileges most prisoners never had, and more privileges than my ancestors had in enslavement.

I often sat out with the mid-wife, an elderly Mexican woman, who spoke only Spanish. I've been grateful for my time in Mexico, learning their culture, customs and, of course, the language.

My baby came into this world a mix of her father and me, a perfect blend. I chose a perfect name too, a name that honored her and the person I named her for. A woman who without her dedication and spirit, my baby and I wouldn't be here. I named her Sara.

My daughter Sara and I stayed incarcerated, mainly for my protection and for her to develop. The soldaderas came to aid me in taking care of the child.

I gave her my breast to suckle on, draining me of my milk whenever it was time. The two of us were inseparable. I taught her everything she needed to know about life, even as an infant.

She grew quicker than I expected. I missed my mother and father and wished she would have gotten to know her grandparents. I made a vow to return to the United States to find them, find some kin, but right now I had an extended family south of the border, who nurtured me and my child.

I needed Robert and Sara needed her father. What a noble father he would make. I imagined him playing with her, teaching her to rope and ride with the best. Where was he? I needed him more than anything. If I heard nothing, I'd go back to Louisiana to find him, along with my kin.

It was April 1865. Sara was now six months old when I heard the news that the war up north ended with a Northern victory. President Lincoln already wrote the Emancipation Proclamation to free enslaved people like my family and myself. Other escapees and I living in Mexico celebrated the end of the war, but many were worried.

Former escapees danced, drank and hollered. "We're free. We're free. We can go home." Some plotted their return. Others remained cautious. Julius, an older man, and one of the first escapees from Louisiana to settle in Mexico had more sobering thoughts.

The mentor sucked his tobacco through a corncob pipe and picked a banjo similar to what Daddy used to play in our cabin. The man never looked up but spoke to us freed people with eloquence with his straw hat pulled over his eyes.

"We ain't ever gonna be free up there. They gonna hate us even more than when they owned us. Those white landowners and their supporters will carry guns and ropes, shooting and hanging us. Nope, we ain't ever gonna be free. They gonna resist all who try to change Louisiana."

The other folks I sat with, stopped to listen, but once the old man finished speaking, they whooped it up again, dancing and screaming. All I knew was I needed Robert, and my kin needed to see my little baby. My husband would soon return from the war. I waited in anticipation.

The year passed by and with their war ended, the war in Mexico escalated but I still was denied combat. The good news was that the United States aided Mexico with weapons and personnel to drive the French out. Could Robert have joined them? I hoped and prayed.

Rebels continued attacking us. Most people knew there would be more internal fighting, so we continued to relocate. Our headquarters moved North in Paso Del Norte, a border town across the Rio Grande from El Paso, Texas. Modern day, Ciudad Juarez.

Sara grew like a weed in the desert. Walking and talking, she became the child others wanted, but still needed her father. Her father needed her. When in heaven would he return? He'd love his daughter.

Chapter 27

April 1866

I received a letter from the United States government. It was in a small, official envelope. The address on it was Washington, D.C. I already knew what it was going to say. Robert had not written or returned any letters in the three and half years he was gone. The only one I received said he joined the Confederacy to avenge his father's and Sara's grandfather's death. I was afraid to open it.

The courier stayed by my side. He had delivered these letters before. A tall, handsome and a maturing Mexican man. He watched me stumble in the act of tearing the paper open.

"It is official," he said in broken English. He patted my shoulder as I read.

KATHERINE BARNUM:

THE LETTER IS TO INFORM YOU OF THE LOSS OF YOUR HUSBAND DURING THE AMERICAN CIVIL WAR.

THEY HUNG ROBERT BARNUM FOR BEING A TRAITOR AND THEFT OF PROPERTY FROM 1858.

I didn't finish reading. I crumpled the paper in a ball and tossed it at the courier, who gave me a hug. Rather than accept the offered comfort, I shoved him aside and raced into the fort which remained my prison. /He had died in the war, but I wondered if he even got a chance to fight for his home. He might have taken out the person who shot his father. At least his life would have come full circle. I would never know. Sara would never meet her father, and I didn't read the entire letter. I did not know where they buried his body, or if he got a proper service.

I looked at Sara, who stumbled towards me. She gave me the most precious hug. I held her tight, refusing to let go of my little girl. A girl born in war, two different wars in neighboring countries.

One was about freedom for a fledgling nation, a nation as young as my daughter. The other a war over the enslavement of my people, a race stolen from their native country and forced into labor. Having families ripped apart and sold to different regions. I was blessed since Master Zeke kept us Turners together during my duration of working his land and in his home. Others were not so lucky; however, we had a sense of community, a sense of strength and bonds, no matter how hard the masters, overseers, and family members tried to break us. We refused to be broken. Zeke Barnum and his peers made a band of stolen and then enslaved people into a force of physical and mental strength. Those fools didn't realize it, and maybe we didn't know it either, but I figured it out as I contemplated my return to Louisiana.

ABOUT THE AUTHOR

Rob Cooke is from Omaha, Nebraska and a graduate from Wayne State College. He is single with three grown children. Cooke is the author of Moonshiner's Legacy, Sara's Swamp Blues, The Lost Song of Miriam Landry, The Tulsa Turnaround, and The End of a Legacy. Cooke's short stories have appeared in various publications including Red Rose Publications, Writers Unite and Sweetycat Productions. Cooke's first love is music and is an editor for The Blues Society of Omaha.